DOM

KV-389-265

**Library at Home Service**
Community Services
Hounslow Library, CentreSpace
24 Treaty Centre, High Street
Hounslow TW3 1ES

YOUR COMMUNITY
YOUR SERVICES

| 0 | 1 | 2 | 3 | 4 | 5 | 6 | 7 | 8 | 9 | LL |
|---|---|---|---|---|---|---|---|---|---|---|
| 780 | 861 | 402 | | 944 | 555 058 | 446 | 887 | 818 | 929 | |
| | | | 693 net | | | | 3087 | | 7559 | |
| 870 | | | 364 | 995 | | | 367 | | 9529 | |
| 870 | | | 723 | | 3325 | 3457 | | | | |
| | | | 7803 | | | 346 507 | | 1588 | | |
| | | | 833 | | | | | 3308 | | |
| | | | 943 | | | | | | | |
| | | | | | | | | | | |
| | | | | | | | | | | |
| | | | | | | | | | | |
| | | | | | | | | | | |
| | | | | | | | | | | |

LIBRARY AT HOME SERVICE
COMMUNITY SERVICES
HOUNSLOW LIBRARY
CENTRESPACE
24 TREATY CENTRE
HIGH ST HOUNSLOW. TW3 1ES
TEL 0845 456 2800

P10-L-2061

C0000 002 025 871

# SPECIAL MESSAGE TO READERS

This book is published by

## THE ULVERSCROFT FOUNDATION

a registered charity in the U.K., No. 264873

The Foundation was established in 1974 to provide funds to help towards research, diagnosis and treatment of eye diseases. Below are a few examples of contributions made by THE ULVERSCROFT FOUNDATION:

A new Children's Assessment Unit
at Moorfield's Hospital, London.
•
Twin operating theatres at the
Western Ophthalmic Hospital, London.
•
The Frederick Thorpe Ulverscroft Chair of
Ophthalmology at the University of Leicester.
•
Eye Laser equipment to various eye hospitals.

If you would like to help further the work of the Foundation by making a donation or leaving a legacy, every contribution, no matter how small, is received with gratitude. Please write for details to:

## THE ULVERSCROFT FOUNDATION,
### The Green, Bradgate Road, Anstey, Leicester LE7 7FU. England
### Telephone: (0533)364325

Love is
a time of enchantment:
in it all days are fair and all fields
green. Youth is blest by it,
old age made benign:
the eyes of love see
roses blooming in December,
and sunshine through rain. Verily
is the time of true-love
a time of enchantment — and
Oh! how eager is woman
to be bewitched!

# HER PART OF THE HOUSE

Artist Jonny won a prize which gave him free art tuition in Italy for a year, but he had to have a wife. On a common sense basis only, he asked Emma to marry him, not guessing that she loved him to distraction. Emma agreed, insisting that they both had their own parts of the house when they married but hoping that in that year he would come to love her too.

*Books by Mary Raymond*
*in the Ulverscroft Large Print Series:*

GRANDMA TYSON'S LEGACY
CHANGE OF HEART
ISLAND OF THE HEART
THAT SUMMER
TAKE-OVER
SHADOW OF A STAR

| L. B. HOUNSLOW LARGE PRINT COLLECTION | |
|---|---|
| SITE | DATE |
| 1 DOM | 07/02 |
| 2 | |
| 3 | |
| 4 | |
| 5 | |

MARY RAYMOND

---- ◆ ----

# HER PART
# OF
# THE HOUSE

*Complete and Unabridged*

# ULVERSCROFT
*Leicester*

First published in Great Britain in 1960


First Large Print Edition
published May 1993


Copyright © 1960 by Mary Raymond
All rights reserved

British Library CIP Data

Raymond, Mary
    Her part of the house.—Large print ed.—
Ulverscroft large print series: romance
I. Title
823.914 [F]


ISBN 0–7089–2866–8

Published by
F. A. Thorpe (Publishing) Ltd.
Anstey, Leicestershire

Set by Words & Graphics Ltd.
Anstey, Leicestershire
Printed and bound in Great Britain by
T. J. Press (Padstow) Ltd., Padstow, Cornwall

This book is printed on acid-free paper

# 1

THE shuffling and scuffling among the horde of boys round the art room door subsided as Emma appeared at the head of the stairs.

A chorus of voices greeted her. "Sir's gone, Miss Leigh!" "Mr. Brereton rushed off half an hour ago, Miss Leigh!" "Sir's not here, Miss Leigh!"

Emma looked down into their varied faces, grimy and ink-stained after the day's strenuous tussle with learning. They were demons and she knew it, and they knew she knew it.

"What are you all doing here?" she asked briskly, hiding her disappointment from these many sharp eyes. She hadn't seen Jonny properly for days. "It's after four. Don't you want to go home?"

Oh, yes, they wanted to go home, they were just clearing up, they were just on the point of departure. Their replies came in a quick cluster.

"Mr. Brereton had to leave half an

hour before art class finished," piped up Grant Minor, a small thin boy, one of Jonny's star pupils. "He had an important appointment, he said. He left me to lock up."

"You mean you were left alone for half an hour?" asked Emma.

Jonny was mad, of course, and the head would be madder if he knew. You couldn't leave a class of ten-and eleven-year-olds alone in a studio for half an hour. What a lovely time they must have had sloshing paint at each other. No wonder they looked even more stained than usual.

"I think I had better look inside the art room," Emma said. The boys parted for her and then trooped into the big airy studio at her heels.

Emma looked round her with a critical eye but the studio did not seem any more untidy than was customary.

"Okay," she said, "I misjudged you."

"Well, you see, we did clear up, Miss Leigh," said Grant Minor.

"Good, good," Emma said, "now lock up as Mr. Brereton told you to."

She went down the stairs, her high

heels clicking on the wooden boards. She wondered where Jonny had gone in such a rush but then she was always wondering where Jonny was, or where he was going, and sometimes with whom he was. She seemed to have been wondering about Jonny for most of her life.

The headmaster was still in his study when she put her head round the door to see if there was anything else for her to do. "Ask Mr. Brereton to come and see me before he leaves," the head said. "I want to ask him about those posters he's supposed to be doing for the swimming gala."

"Mr. Brereton has just this minute gone," said Emma quickly, protectively.

The head looked at his watch. "Gets away right on time, doesn't he?" he remarked.

His tone was dry but not acrimonious. He was a sweet man, her boss, Emma reflected and a kind and clever one with a marvellously tolerant understanding of small boys. She liked working for him as his secretary. The prep. school was a world in miniature and she was absorbed by it.

Not so Jonny Brereton, the art master. Teaching small boys to draw was not Jonny's idea of pleasant work. He had serious pretensions as a painter. He would have liked to paint all day long and live on the smell of turpentine. But he had a widowed mother to support. By working as an art master, he achieved some sort of compromise. He was able to keep his mother, although he was always hard up, and he also had some free time in the long school holidays to paint and to study and to travel (he had hitch-hiked his way all over Europe and North Africa, for instance).

"I'll see Mr. Brereton sometime to-morrow then," the headmaster said. "You may go, Miss Leigh, I think we're all clear."

Emma went into her own small office and put on her coat and combed her hair, looking into the mirror behind the cupboard door.

She looked at her reflection without much interest. She was slight and not very tall and always felt undistinguished and unnoticeable. She had a tall, blonde, very pretty sister who had always attracted the first attention of strangers. In her shadow Emma had never thought of herself as pretty or indeed as anything much.

She combed her hair away from her face and pinned it back. It was thick and silky and the colour of a moth's wing. Or so Jonny had once described it. Or a mouse, as Emma had answered.

"A lucky mouse," Jonny had grinned back, "to be so sleek and shiny." She could see his face as he said it. Not strictly handsome, hawk-nosed, vivid, with the black eyes and the black hair which fell constantly over his forehead. Febrile was a word Emma had once applied to Jonny without actually knowing exactly what it meant. When afterwards, she looked it up in the dictionary, she discovered it was a fancy substitute for feverish. It was a true description. Jonny was consumed with a fever. He whirled away, febrile, mercurial, excitable, like a dervish, wrapped up in his own vast preoccupations. You could not reach him with yours, except occasionally. Then he would come out of his private world for a moment. But most of the time he was remote, untrappable, untouchable.

Oh, Jonny. Emma sighed and shut him firmly out of her mind. Going home in the bus, she opened her book and concentrated on *Art from the Nineteenth Century to To-day*. It was a very thick volume which she had got out of the library.

Emma was twenty. She and her elder sister Elizabeth shared a flat together in London. They had been left a little money by their parents but of course they also had to supplement their income by work.

Elizabeth, four years older than Emma, was a fashion model. Tall, slim and beautiful, she was everything that a glamorous model of the first rank should be. She was also warm and generous. Emma loved her dearly. She was never jealous or envious of Elizabeth, or of her multitude of friends, male and female. It seemed to her natural that everyone should love Elizabeth who was as good as she was beautiful.

It was Elizabeth now who opened the door to Emma as she stood outside fumbling for her key among the jumble of things her handbag contained.

Elizabeth stood a moment staring at her with her wide beautiful smile creasing her beautiful face.

"Emma, you must be the first to know. Congratulate me, Stephen and I are engaged!"

In the sitting-room, Emma found Stephen Cunningham, the handsome young barrister who had been one of Elizabeth's more constant escorts during the past few months. Emma had thought that perhaps Elizabeth had been quite keen on him, but beneath Elizabeth's general gaiety and high spirits, she had never detected any real burning emotion. But she had been wrong. Elizabeth looked more beautiful than ever with happiness. She and Stephen were both radiant with their love.

Emma felt affected as she looked at them. She felt some of their glow must surely rub on to her.

Elizabeth was bubbling over with plans. They were going to get married very soon. There was no reason to wait. They were sure of one another. Stephen had a very pleasant flat which was big enough for two.

It was June. They were going down to the country, driving in Stephen's Jaguar. Elizabeth was taking two weeks off so that she could meet Stephen's people. They lived in the Cotswolds in an old manor house where the Cunninghams had lived for generations. Everything was marvellous. Only one thing worried Elizabeth. She said so.

"It's you, Emma," she looked down at her younger sister. Emma gazed back at her.

"How will you manage without me?" Elizabeth went on. "I mean with the rent of the flat. It will be too much for you on your own."

Emma sighed. "I'll manage somehow," she said vaguely. "I'll get a lodger, or a girl friend to share."

It was only when they had gone and she was wandering round the empty flat that the full impact of the change in her life hit her. Elizabeth was getting married. From now on, she would be on her own. She went over to the record player and put on some records at random. This was not much help. The first one which clicked and fell with

8

a plop on to the turn-table was Louis Armstrong's 'Mack the Knife.' This was old but it was one of Jonny's favourites. It conjured up his face, his voice, his presence so strongly that he might almost have been in the room. She could see him tapping his foot, husking out the words, with the little actions to suit them '*The line forms on the right, dear . . .* '

Emma sat down suddenly on a low chair and put her face in her hands, "Oh, Jonny," she whispered. If only she and Jonny were getting married! She felt the hot tears sting her eyelids and got up and ran into her bedroom and flung herself on the bed, sobbing uncontrollably. They were tears of self-pity, she knew, despicable tears, but she could not help herself. She was happy for Elizabeth, happy for her with her nice Stephen. She had never really been jealous of Elizabeth but why did everything have to work so smoothly for her? She fell in love and she got engaged and she was going to be married. Soon because the young man was the right age, with the right income. She would have a lovely wedding and a lovely home

9

afterwards, and then she would produce two lovely babies, first a boy and then a girl. It would be like a fairy story.

'But I'm — I'm like one of those children who never had any of the good fairies at their christening,' thought Emma wildly. 'I fall in love, too young, with a man who thinks of me first as a kid, and then as a useful stick of furniture about the place and even if Jonny were in love with me, we could never be married because he's too poor anyway.' But if only he loved her! She'd wait years for him. She had waited years for him, four long years to be precise. Once she had thought she would get over it, but not any more. She was stuck with Jonny Brereton for keeps.

She had cried so much that she felt she hadn't a drop of moisture left in her body. She got up off the bed and dabbed at her face ineffectually with a tissue. She pulled a grimace at herself in the glass. "You look hideous," she told her reflection and she went into the kitchen and made herself a cup of coffee and spread a piece of brown wholemeal bread with thick butter and a lot of pickles.

She was eating this concoction when she heard a knocking at the front door.

She went on eating the bread and pickles. She couldn't possibly answer the door and see anyone with her eyes all bunged up as they were. The knocking continued and then someone called through the letter-box. It was Jonny Brereton. Emma went on eating. Quietly, like a mouse, she poured herself another cup of coffee. In the end, Jonny went away. A few minutes later, the phone rang.

It was Jonny. He was in a call-box round the corner. "I knew you were in," he said. "I could see the light. I've got to see you, Emma. It's very urgent."

When he arrived the second time, he said without preamble, "I've won a prize — the Margaret Grasselli prize in Florence!"

Emma stared at him. "What's that?" she asked. "I've never heard of it."

"It's a grant of money for a year's study in Florence and Rome, and any other parts of Italy I want to visit," said Jonny impatiently.

Emma broke into exclamations of

congratulation and pleasure at his good fortune. But there was a little hollow feeling inside her at the implications of his news. "There's something else as well," Jonny said, "I've also got a portrait commission."

"We-ell," Emma stepped back. "Come into the sitting-room and tell me all about it."

"You remember those portraits I had in the Young Artists of Promise show at the Warwick Galleries," Jonny began.

Emma nodded. She had powdered and made up her face. Her eyes were still puffed up, but if Jonny noticed she had been crying, he did not waste time on remarking it aloud.

"Well," went on Jonny, "they apparently caught the fancy of an Italian gent called Ugo Grasselli. This Grasselli knows old Graham — "

"Graham who?"

"Professor Maxwell Graham. You know, my old art master at the London — he's always believed in my talent as a painter."

"Oh, yes," said Emma.

"Well, then, this Ugo Grasselli knows

12

Graham and asked his advice. Apparently, Ugo Grasselli had an English wife, Margaret, who was very interested in the arts, and when she died, which was some years ago, she left a sum of money to be devoted to the interests of young English painters. Ugo Grasselli himself added to the fund, and he is the head of a small committee which administers it. The chosen painter is provided with board and lodging plus expenses money for a year's study in Italy. Ugo Grasselli asked Professor Graham for some names and Graham thought of me, but as soon as he suggested my name, Grasselli remembered it too, because you see he'd seen my portraits. It was one of those amazing, fateful coincidences. In addition to which, Grasselli wants me to paint his beautiful daughter, also teach her as she has apparently the most enormous talent herself."

Jonny helped himself to some coffee and then went on, "It all sounds wonderful. The Grassellis live in Florence so I'd probably spend some time there first, with all those marvellous masterpieces all round me to go and look at, and in addition to my board and lodging, I'd have some money in my pocket, and I'd be working in that beautiful, limpid Italian light. I would leave as soon as school breaks up."

"So you're going to Italy for a year," said Emma. It was the end of the world. "How very nice for you." She felt as if she were going to die. Not to see Jonny for a whole year! How was she going to be able to bear it. This news, on top of Elizabeth's engagement, was almost more than she could stand. She wished she could give vent to her feelings, but she sat steadily in her armchair, her legs curled beneath her, talking as tranquilly as though Jonny were discussing a trip to Bournemouth.

"It's not as simple as all that," said Jonny, "I've been to see Grasselli this afternoon. I left school early. He's staying at the Dorchester, over here on some business. He's an importer or something. There is a condition attached to the bequest. The prize winner must be married. Margaret Grasselli had some theory that a married artist would concentrate more on his work. All the

14

domestic side of his life would be taken care of. Absolute rubbish, of course. One can always find someone to sew one's buttons on."

"Perhaps that was what she had in mind," said Emma dryly. "Maybe she wanted to make sure her artist would live in a proper ménage and not a rag-tag and bobtail one."

"I've got to take a chance on the Grasselli girl's portrait," Jonny went on. "He will only pay me if he likes it."

"But how can you accept the prize?" asked Emma. "You're not married."

"No," said Jonny, "I'm not married." He paused a moment and then gave her a sidelong look. "But I said I was."

"You're mad," said Emma, "hasn't your wife got to go too?"

"Of course," said Jonny.

Emma stared at him.

Jonny looked at her directly. "I said my wife's name was Emma," he said.

Emma sat up. Her heart was beating uncontrollably. "Jonathan Brereton, are you out of your mind? What an extraordinary proposal!"

"I'm not asking you to marry me, you

15

ass," said Jonny, "although I must say you needn't sound so astonished about it," he added with sarcasm. "I'd probably make some girl an excellent husband. I'm asking you to come to Italy and *pretend* you are my wife!"

Emma leaned back in her chair. She was sick with disappointment. How absurd her heart was, to leap with pleasure like that at the idea that Jonny was proposing to her in an unromantic but roundabout fashion. At all costs, she must not let Jonny see how distressed she was at her mistake.

"You are absolutely ridiculous," she said. "How could I pretend to be your wife? Our passports would give the game away."

Jonny stood up and came and sat on the arm of her chair. "Look, dearest Emma, I have it all worked out. We travel together, only when we get to Italy do we pretend we are married and even then we only have to pretend to the Grassellis and their friends. You know me well enough to trust me like your brother. It will be marvellous for you too. You'll be able to wander round Florence and look at all those treasures. Then, later on, there will be Rome. Please, please, Emma, do this for me. Think what it means to me. You know how difficult life always is. It'll be a godsend to be able to make some money, with the opportunity of making more, and get kept and fed into the bargain for a whole year. I'll be able to send Mother away for a breath of sea air. It will be of mutual benefit. You'll adore Italy."

"There's my job — " Emma began.

"Oh, phooey about your job," Jonny broke in impatiently. "The old boy will have plenty of time to find another secretary, and another art master — two and a half months to be precise — we wouldn't leave before the end of this term anyway."

Emma was silent. Jonny had no need to be so eloquent. The vistas he conjured up were breathtaking in their promise of pleasure and happiness. To be close to Jonny, to be his companion for a whole year, to be in new, exciting surroundings, what more had the world to offer?

"What are you afraid of?" asked Jonny. He stood up and began pacing about the room. "This is not an improper suggestion. You know you can trust me. I have watched you grow up. When have I ever made a pass at you?"

Emma laughed, as she always did with Jonny, to hide her mixture of feelings. "But you have always been Elizabeth's friend."

Jonny paused in his tracks and looked at her. "But I was — I am — a friend of you both."

Emma glanced at him: '*But you liked Elizabeth best,*' she thought, '*I was always the little kid sister tagging along.*'

She laughed again and said, "To be perfectly honest, I always thought you were one of Elizabeth's lame ducks. You know how she collects them."

"I have never been a lame duck in my life," Jonny sounded both surprised and furious.

"Oh," said Emma airily, pleased that she had stirred him to some show of feeling, "all Elizabeth's lame ducks turn out to be swans. There was that man who did the marvellous fruit and flower pictures — he certainly bit the hand that fed him — and there was Ronny

Sayre who went to Hollywood and wrote all those terrifically successful scripts . . . You must admit you were pretty down in the dumps when she found you."

"You were pretty down in the dumps yourselves," said Jonny slowly and gently. "It was just after your parents had died very sadly within a month of each other. Remember? I admit Elizabeth helped me — she believed in my talent when few others did and it was inspiring. But I thought I also helped her, and you. You were sixteen and she was twenty. You both seemed pretty much a couple of babes in the wood."

"You did help us," Emma said warmly, suddenly contrite. Why did she always say things to Jonny she didn't really mean? It was a defensive habit she had. Rather than let him know how much she adored and loved him, she would prefer him to think her off-hand and unappreciative. "I'm only teasing you," she added. "You were wonderful to us." He *had* been wonderful. That bad time was the foundation of her affection. In their sudden bereavement, they had had no uncles and aunts, no near relatives to sustain them. There were older friends, of course, contemporaries of their parents who had been shocked by the sudden tragedy and who had been kind. But it was Jonny, whom Elizabeth had met through work, who had been the most understanding, the most helpful, the most truly sympathetic, perhaps because although not much older than they, his own life had been difficult since his schooldays.

That had been four years ago and he had been in their lives ever since. He lived only just around the corner, he was in and out of their home constantly. His mother lived in the country with her sister and while he went often enough to see her, it was Elizabeth who often mended his socks and told him to buy himself some more shirts as his present ones were 'positively disgustingly old.'

At first, Emma had assumed that, like so many others, he was in love with Elizabeth, but apparently it was not so or else he got over it quickly. Perhaps he just liked the relaxed family atmosphere they provided. They had a lot of shared jokes. Some nights he would come over and help them cook the supper and wash up and play records, and not talk at all very much. Other nights he would be on a talking jag and would tell them all his ideas and how he would accomplish them.

In the time they knew him he went through a lot of girl friends. Emma suffered as each one joined their circle for a long or shortish period and then disappeared into limbo, never to be heard of again. He was not like Elizabeth who seemed to be able to transmute her most ardent admirers into tranquil friends.

Jonny's girls were all kinds — there was Varina, an exotic fashion model from Paris whom Elizabeth had worked with and who had eyes like a Persian princess. There was a blonde artist with long yellow hair and red stockings who didn't wash enough. There was Angela who hunted and wore cashmere sweaters and pearls. His taste was catholic but they all had one thing in common. They were raving beauties. Jonny was very susceptible to beauty. Or so Emma had decided.

"There's a lot of the mother in Elizabeth," Jonny said now. "She likes taking care of people. You and I are going to miss her. We are the kind who have to be taken care of."

"I don't think she will have to take care of Stephen," said Emma stiffly. "He will be looking after her."

"You like your future brother-in-law, don't you?" Jonny said.

"Very much." Emma reached out and helped herself to a cigarette. Her hand trembled slightly as she put it to her lips.

Jonny flicked open his lighter with a quick gesture and reached forward. Emma had difficulty with her cigarette. She could feel him staring at her but steadily refused to meet his eyes.

"Don't you like him?" she asked at last, blowing out a stream of smoke in an off-hand manner.

"He's okay," Jonny said. "I'm never in tune with those terribly correct, good school, better university types. Stephen doesn't seem quite real to me."

"You sound jealous," Emma said lightly.

Jonny snorted. "Don't be absurd. I'm glad Elizabeth has found someone she loves so much. I adore Elizabeth. I am proud to have her as my friend. But she is not the type I find attractive. I mean I love looking at her. She is very decorative but I have never had a desire to catch hold of her. She might break. You're much more the type of girl I'd consider cuddling. But you don't have to worry about that. This is a business proposition."

He looked at her pleadingly. "Come with me to Italy," he said softly, "and do everyone a good turn — me, my mother and yourself."

Emma looked into his black eyes and was lost. Who knew what might happen in Italy? She gave way to temptation and said with sudden decision, "Okay, I'll come, but don't let us tell anyone that we are going to pretend to be married."

Jonny gave her a quick bear hug and an enormous kiss on the side of her cheek. "You're an angel, a darling, and I love you, in a manner of speaking," he cried. "Of course we won't tell anyone, silly girl. We'll tell them that I have won this prize, that you have been offered a job teaching English. No one will think it odd. We'll give our notice in at the school this week . . ."

But if she had said she was going to work for a family of gorillas instead of the Grassellis, Emma did not think Elizabeth would have heard or noticed. She was wrapped in a rosy dream world of her marriage plans. All she wanted to be sure of was that Emma would delay her departure until the wedding.

The next few weeks were a kind of phantasmagoria in Emma's memory. There were the frenzied preparations for the wedding, the wedding itself, her own packing, their plans for the flat.

They were lucky about the flat. They were able to let it furnished to a nice young couple who had been posted to London from the Midlands for a year.

Elizabeth's and Stephen's wedding was over, they were on their honeymoon, her own packing was done, and Emma was busy with the house agent over the inventory of the flat one morning when Jonny came in and said that the plans for their trip to Italy were off.

Emma looked up from the long typed list of furniture which the house agent had made. She stared at Jonny.

"What do you mean?"

"It's no good," Jonny said morosely, "we can't go."

He slouched about the room, his hands in his pockets, taking no notice of the house agent. "The whole thing is too complicated."

"Would you mind waiting, Jonny, while I get this inventory done with Mr. Sims? I've nearly finished."

"It's a waste of time," Jonny said. He flung himself into a chair. "You won't be leaving the flat after all."

Emma turned her back on him. "I think we've finished here, Mr. Sims," she said sweetly. "Let's do the kitchen."

When she had got rid of Mr. Sims at last, she went into Jonny and demanded, "What is all this?"

From the depths of the chair, Jonny looked up at her. "Oh, it's all too difficult," he said. "I've discovered we've got to show our passports, the Margaret Grasselli prize people want all sorts of papers which you'll have to sign — it's all too risky — we'd get found out — and besides — " he paused.

"Besides what?"

Jonny hesitated a moment. "Oh, I suppose it sounds corny and old-fashioned, but I can't let you do it. I can't let you throw yourself away for a whole year on me. I was mad ever to contemplate it. It's just that this prize — this grant — is such a marvellous opportunity, opening so many vistas — Ugo Grasselli says there is a chance of my having an exhibition in Rome at the end of the year — and I suppose I couldn't let it go by. The idea was born of desperation."

Emma stared at him in desolation. She was bitterly, uncontrollably disappointed.

After a pause, Jonny went on, "And there are other reasons, though that is the most important. If we were found out, as we might well be, it would have very unpleasant repercussions. It's false pretences for one thing — and it's dishonest for another. I am robbing another man who *is* married and who is probably as worthy of the grant as I. No, darling Emma, I'm afraid our wonderful trip to cloud cuckoo land is off." He got up and went over to the window.

Emma said quietly addressing his back, "There *is* one way in which we could go properly and legally."

Jonny turned around. He had been staring disconsolately down into the street. "And which way is that?" he asked.

"We could get married," the words were barely a whisper. At his look of surprise, Emma went on hurriedly, "Oh, I mean on the same basis as before. I know there is nothing romantic between us. It could still be a business proposition. It would be a very workable arrangement. We get on well enough. I could run your house, perhaps teach, you could do your studying. We could get married in a registry office and after the year was up, we could go our separate ways."

But perhaps, a voice whispered to her heart, perhaps after a year you might love me, perhaps after a year you might have got accustomed to my face, perhaps after a year you might not want to go your separate way.

"You're a funny girl, Emma," Jonny said slowly. "Would you do that for me?"

"Not for you entirely," said Emma coolly. "It means a trip abroad, and I've hardly been out of England. I'm going to be on my own anyway, now that Elizabeth is married. That was why I agreed to go with you in the first place. It would be a terrible disappointment to me if we didn't go." She laughed a little shakily. "And think of the inconvenience — I've given up my job, and the lease of the flat has been signed . . . I've done all my packing . . . !"

Jonny said slowly, "The Margaret Grasselli prize is worth nearly a thousand pounds in cash and kind — it sounds astronomical in lira. It's a crazy idea, Emma, but we'll do it. We'll take a chance and hope for the best!"

"It doesn't have to be a proper marriage," said Emma stiffly. "I mean, it's purely a business deal. I don't want you to think — "

"You don't have to labour the point," Jonny said, his manner a little grim. "I got what you meant the first time. I won't leap into your bed at the first opportunity and demand my conjugal rights, if that's what you are afraid of."

Emma's face flamed. "Oh, Jonny," she said.

"I understand perfectly, Emma," Jonny went on smoothly, his bright eyes on her face noticing the flush. "Any amorous advances or attentions on my part are strictly not wanted, but what makes you think I would proffer them? Or do you know me so well that you think I might, in an idle moment, when I have nothing better to do?"

The flush had receded from Emma's face, leaving her very pale. "I am sure I would never be in any danger," she said with spirit, "I could never hope to compete with any of your girl friends, especially that yellow-haired one with the dirty neck."

Jonny gave a sudden shout of laughter. "Emma, Emma," he cried, "you're worth a dozen of my girl friends. I promise we'll have fun!"

★ ★ ★

But the fun, thought Emma, as she dressed for her wedding day, was a long time in coming.

They were being married in the local registry office, by special licence. They had told no one of their plans, not even Jonny's mother. That had been his idea.

"Let's just keep it to ourselves," he begged, "I couldn't stand any kind of hoo-ha and exclamations of astonishment at the rush. We'll write and tell everyone from Italy."

Emma acquiesced. Of course he wanted it kept quiet because it was a marriage of convenience and nothing to get excited about, and the quieter the beginning, the less fuss over the end when the time came for them to part. In any case, although there were friends she would have liked to have told, Elizabeth was far away in Spain and not easily available since she and Stephen were touring.

In keeping with the casual nature of the occasion, Emma at first decided to buy nothing new to wear, and then suddenly at the last minute she changed her mind. Why not pretend she was a proper bride and do it for luck? She rushed round the shops and bought herself a pale blue dress. It was expensive and very becoming to her, bringing out the deep blue of her eyes, flattering her fair skin. And it would be useful in Italy. With a small white scrap of a hat, white shoes, gloves and bag, she thought she looked presentable enough on the morning of her wedding.

Just before she finished dressing, a florist's messenger came round with a tight Victorian posy, complete with lacy frill and long pink satin ribbons. It was composed of pink and dark red roses and gardenias, and as Emma put her nose to it, its perfume came up to meet her like incense. With it there was a note from Jonny. With trembling fingers, Emma tore it open. 'Just to remind you. Love from Jonny.'

Emma managed to smile at the terse little note. She looked at the posy again. It was beautiful. She felt sure Jonny had chosen the flowers himself because that was the sort of thing he always did. She felt nervous suddenly and wished she could go to sleep and wake up when it was all over.

Jonny came round for her in a taxi a little while afterwards. In his dark formal suit, he did not look like himself. Emma was so accustomed to his haphazard ways of dressing — even on formal occasions, he was quite likely to wear a brightly checked shirt with a tie — that she had half expected him to turn up in his usual attire of jeans or slacks, open shirt and rough sweater. Instead, he wore his well-cut best suit, a white silk shirt, and a very subdued hand-knitted tie. He had had an impeccable shave and his hair was slicked back. As he stood there, looking so attractive and bold and assured and so distinguished, Emma had to turn away in case he saw the unbridled admiration in her eyes.

He caught hold of her hands and pulled her round to face him. "Don't go shy on me, now," he said. Emma felt herself flushing and stared up at him with difficulty. He looked her up and down and then turned her round.

"Why, Emma!" he said, and there seemed to be a kind of surprise in his voice. "You look like a bride!" His eyes were bright and mocking.

Emma disengaged herself from his hands. "You look quite presentable yourself," she said coldly. "In fact, I have never seen you look so civilised. You should get married more often."

"So should you," Jonny said. "It suits you."

They both laughed and Emma realised with a little shock of surprise that Jonny was nervous too.

In the taxi going to the registry office, they were both silent. Clutching her posy as though it were a life-belt, Emma could not help remembering Elizabeth's wedding, less than two short weeks ago. Up to now, she had restrained herself from making comparisons, but as she and Jonny drove through the sunny streets, the memories came pouring into her mind. Elizabeth had been the fairy-tale bride, in a gorgeous white dress given to her by one of the couturiers for whom she had worked regularly, and the church, a small fashionable one in Knightsbridge, had been packed with all her and Stephen's friends and all the Cunningham relations. And there had been the reception afterwards at the hotel with champagne and a buffet lunch. Emma's mind dwelt for a moment on the hundred and one wedding presents she had received. The flat had been awash with tissue paper. Emma shut the memories firmly away at the back of her mind. She was stupid to compare the two occasions. And, after all, she was getting her dearest wish. She was marrying Jonny. She had a whole year to prove herself, to make herself indispensable to him. But oh, she added despairingly, how do you make yourself indispensable to a man who is so invulnerable? She sympathised with all the girls of the olden days who had believed in love philtres. Oh, if only she had a potion to give Jonny! "We'll have to get a couple of witnesses off the street," said Jonny suddenly.

Emma came out of her reverie with a start. She had not thought about witnesses. In the end, they did not have passers-by but the best man and the matron of honour of the couple who were to be married after them, and who had arrived too early.

The registrar was a little man with enormously thick spectacles. He was both solemn and precise and when they had made their protestations, he picked up a pen and said, "Please sign here, Mrs. Brereton," as though getting her new name out as quickly as possible was all part of the ceremony.

"Don't look so solemn," Jonny said looking at Emma, "it's not for keeps, sweetheart, or a prison sentence."

The registrar looked pained for a moment and then presumed Jonny was making some feeble sort of a joke and smiled at them both.

He shook hands with them and wished them luck, and the two witnesses, a Mr. James Brand, and a Mrs. Brownie Whittaker, also shook hands and wished them luck. Well, they're certainly ships in the night, thought Emma, in some way touched by these good wishes from strangers, I don't suppose we'll see Mr. Brand or Mrs. Whittaker ever again in our whole lives.

As she and Jonny walked out of the registry office, a photographer who had been lurking in the hallway stepped forward. He took two quick pictures and a girl who was with him came up to them and took Jonny's address. "We'll send you prints," she promised.

"Was that your idea?" asked Jonny as they walked into the street.

Emma shook her head. "I think some of these wedding photographers work on spec," she said, secretly pleased that there was going to be a photograph to treasure.

Jonny hailed a cab and told the driver to go to the Savoy. He sank back into his seat. "Well, that's that," he said.

"You sound as if you have been to the dentist," said Emma.

"I must say I thought it was about as grim," Jonny said. "Anyway let's forget it, Emma, and have a lunch to celebrate our departure to Italy this evening."

With their lunch of smoked salmon and chicken, he ordered champagne, and the wine loosened the tension between them and they began to talk and laugh. Emma's heart was beating unaccountably hard. Now they really were at the beginning of their adventure.

★ ★ ★

They took the night ferry to France. Jonny had booked them a sleeper in the train which was to take them to Paris where they had to change for a train which would take them to Italy. They were both tired and exhausted when they arrived in France and when they had found their carriage, which they had to themselves, Jonny said, "I suggest we try and get some sleep right away," and Emma agreed.

She unpacked her small case and took out her flannel and toothbrush and went to the bathroom to wash and clean her teeth.

When she came back, Jonny had made up their bunks and stowed away their luggage.

"Which bunk would you like?" he asked. "Maybe the bottom one would be more comfortable for you."

He took his own towel and toothbrush and went off.

When he came back, Emma had changed into a pink and white candy striped cotton housecoat, also part of her 'trousseau'. She had propped her mirror on the top bunk and was brushing her hair.

She turned as Jonny slid the door back

and came into the carriage. Their eyes met for a long moment as though they were two strangers who had never seen each other before.

"You look about ten years old with no make-up," Jonny observed at length and began loosening his tie. He had already taken off his jacket and hung it up.

"Let me get out of your way," said Emma, quickly picking up her mirror. She looked at him warily. Jonny's eyes were hard as he stared back at her. "Okay, Emma," he said, "stop looking as scared as a maiden aunt who's found a man under her bed. I'm not going to bite you." He leaned forward and brushed her forehead casually with his lips. "Sleep well, Emma," he said, "good night."

"Good night," Emma said, and lay down on her own bunk and drew her blanket over her.

In a few moments, Jonny was in his own bunk above her head and they were lying in darkness.

But as the train rumbled through the night with the alien sound of a French train, Emma lay wide awake. She was completely exhausted but she could not sleep. Jonny's last words smarted in her memory.

Maiden aunt indeed! She felt he knew his power over her — that he had guessed it long ago — that he could make her flush with embarrassment as he willed, unnerve her with a glance, annoy her with a word and swing her to heights of expectation with another.

It was no good. She must control her emotions. She must not put the weapon in his hand. Jonny could be cruel. It would bore him and embarrass him if he knew the extent of her feelings about him, feelings he could not obviously return since he compared her to a ten-year-old child one minute and a maiden aunt the next! Besides, she had seen the way he had treated those of his girl friends who had been importunate after their dismissal from his life. He had never been kind to them, ever.

She thought, 'I would have married him on any terms — these terms or any other terms — but he must never know that.' What happiness could there be in it for her? She wanted Jonny's love as well as his passion, his fidelity as well as his friendship. I wish I were as beautiful as Cleopatra, Emma thought wildly. I wish when I wake up I could be like Venus rising from the foam and stun him. She smiled faintly in the darkness at the thought of a stunned Jonny. She could not imagine him either suppliant or humble, only taking what he wanted when he wanted.

She slept fitfully and arose unrefreshed and they had a mad scramble to wash and get dressed and catch their train for Italy. It proved to be crowded and although they found their reserved seats, the corridors were packed with garlic-scented, garrulous Italian labourers going home.

As their train came into the station at Florence, Emma, after the long, hot, uncomfortable journey, had never felt so tired and bedraggled. She longed for both bed and bath. She was completely bemused by the foreign scene and the foreign tongues around her and felt as if she had been travelling for thousands of hours.

Jonny, however, seemed to have been

stimulated by the journey, tiresome though he agreed it had been.

"Ugo Grasselli said he would meet us!" he said, and hung out of the window. In a few minutes, Emma saw him wave animatedly. Obviously, he had spotted Grasselli among the crowds on the platform.

When Emma herself was on the platform a little while later, she discovered that Ugo Grasselli was accompanied by his daughter Paola.

Jonny introduced his wife and they all gravely shook hands. Ugo Grasselli was a short plump man with benign brown eyes and crisp white hair. His daughter Paola was taller than he was. She was very slim with a clear fair skin, presumably inherited from her English mother, now burned to an apricot hue by the sun. Her hair was light brown with gold flecks in it and her eyes were huge and brown.

As she stood there beside her father, looking cool and exquisite, in a crisply fresh, dazzling cotton frock, Emma thought she had never seen anything more beautiful. No wonder her father wants her painted, she thought. In the dusty, hot, atmosphere of the station, she seemed like a being from another world.

Emma, conscious of her crumpled dress and feeling dirty and unkempt, smiled as best she might.

"We have our car," Paola said in careful, accented English. Her wonderful eyes were on Jonny. Jonny was looking right back at her, Emma noted, and her heart gave a painful lurch. She remembered that he was going to teach as well as paint the beautiful Paola.

"Your little house is all ready for you," said Ugo Grasselli. "Paola has been very busy with the arrangements. Now let us see about your luggage."

# 2

THE Grasselli villa was a few miles outside Florence set in beautiful gardens and the whole estate surrounded by rolling farmland whose peach orchards, vineyards and olive groves were also part of Ugo Grasselli's interests.

"Paola says we are buried in the country," he said as they drove along, "but I think we have the best of both worlds. We are not very far from Florence where I have my business and yet we also have fresh air. That is very important in the heat of the summer."

He swerved to avoid a farm-cart moving slowly along the narrow, straight, tree-lined road.

"As I think I told you in London," Ugo Grasselli went on, "you are free to stay here as long as you choose, move off to Rome or any other place whenever you want to. But we only have accommodation ready for you here and in Rome. Elsewhere you will have to find your own board and lodging. But that should not be too difficult. The whole point of the prize is that we do not want any restriction placed on the artist. He does not have to worry about the prosaic details of living. He is free to paint. If he feels like living in a village on a mountain top, he can do so."

"I am very urban," Jonny said. "I think I will prefer Rome and Florence."

Emma looked out of the window, leaving Jonny to make the conversation.

Everywhere she looked she saw a scene or a landscape which she knew and loved. That line of dark cypress, those terraced slopes, the colour of the hills were as familiar to her as her own English countryside, with such faithful love and devotion had Italy's artists depicted their country down the generations and shown its loveliness to the world. She felt as if she had been in Italy before. All that was needed was a group of Renaissance figures in blue and crimson to be posed at the foot of the hills and she would think she was back in the National Gallery.

After about fifteen minutes' drive, they turned in at a pair of gates and up a long curving drive bordered with cypress Emma caught a glimpse of formal gardens, mossy statuary drooping over a dark pool and then the car stopped outside the house with its double staircase flanked with trailing green plants. A white-jacketed servant appeared on the terrace and then came down the steps to greet them.

"I am afraid we will have to walk the rest of the way," said Ugo Grasselli, and he indicated a path leading through the shrubbery at one side of the house.

The late Margaret Grasselli had been something of a painter herself, if a dilettante one, and for her in the gardens her loving husband had built a studio.

The shrubbery was almost a little wood, Emma thought as she followed Ugo Grasselli down the sandy shady path. Behind her followed Paola and Jonny, with the servant Mario bringing up the rear with their suitcases.

They came out of the shade of the trees.

The studio consisted of an enormous

barn-like room with whitewashed walls, hung with paintings left by some of the previous tenants. At one end was a wide minstrel's gallery. Leading up to the gallery was a staircase of wrought-iron and marble. The minstrel's gallery was arranged as a double bedroom with a very luxurious marble-floored and walled bathroom leading off it.

Below, off the studio, was a small kitchen and another bathroom. This attractive studio residence, as a house agent might describe it, was put at the disposal of Mr. and Mrs. Brereton.

"We have always used it as a guest-house," said Paola.

"You will, of course, share our meals," said Ugo Grasselli. "They can be sent over from the house if you do not wish to join us there, and of course our servants will look after you and clean the studio for you. And now I am sure you will want to unpack and have a rest after your journey. Paola and I hope very much you will join us for dinner to-night. Perhaps you would come over to the house at about eight o'clock?"

"Thank you," said Emma.

"I hope you are going to be comfortable," said Paola. She glanced from Emma to Jonny.

"I am sure we are," said Jonny, and Emma smiled her agreement.

Beyond Paola's head against the far white wall of the studio was an extravagant massed arrangement of flowers — tuberoses, zinnias, carnations. The mingled scent of them lay heavy on the air and Emma thought that the sweet perfume would for ever remind her of this moment of arrival and her own mixed emotions of excitement and exhilaration, overlaid with an odd breathless feeling of premonition and foreboding.

"Thank you for the flowers," Emma said, looking at Paola. "They are very beautiful."

Paola gave a little imperceptible shrug as though to dismiss the gorgeousness of this display and followed her father out of the studio.

When they had gone, Jonny caught Emma spontaneously round the waist and danced her round the room, dropping her at last, breathless, on to the couch.

"I feel free," he cried, "marvellously

free. I feel as though I could push down houses — and paint master-pieces!" he added more soberly. "Don't look so solemn, Emma. It is going to do you good too." He looked around for inspiration. "You must learn Italian."

Emma laughed and stood up. She smoothed her crumpled dress. "And I must have a bath and change my clothes. I might feel more human then."

Jonny sat down on the couch she had just vacated. "I suppose we ought to unpack and get ourselves sorted out," he said. He bounced up and down on the couch. "This seems comfortable enough for a bed," he added, his dark eyes on her. "I think I shall sleep here."

"Will you be all right?" Emma asked him a little stiffy.

"Sure, sure," said Jonny cheerfully. "We obviously can't share the bedroom. It's got the most enormous double bed in it. You take over the minstrel's gallery, Emma. That can be your part of the house. You never know, if you're lucky, I might come serenading you one night and you can play Juliet to my Romeo in the balcony scene." He bared his teeth at her in a wide white smile. Emma turned away from his mocking face. Jonny seemed deliberately to want to discomfit her. She walked over to the foot of the staircase and then paused to look at him again. His eyes were still fixed on her, bright, intent, but their expression inscrutable.

"Where is all our luggage?" she asked, the question purposely prosaic and practical.

Jonny shrugged. "I think the man took it all upstairs," he said. "I'll come and collect my suitcase. There's a cupboard in the bathroom down here where I can stow some of my things."

He followed her up the stairs.

The gallery had wide windows at each end and was well fitted with built-in cupboards lined with mirror glass. The bed-covering and the curtains were of the same gaily patterned silk. It was a pretty room as was the pink and black marble bathroom leading off it.

Jonny sorted out his luggage and took his own suitcase and bundle of painting things downstairs again.

Emma went into the bathroom and

ran herself a bath. She tossed in some fragrant essence and had a long comfortable soak.

So! She was in Italy, and married to Jonny. If someone had told her six months ago that this lay in her future, she would have thought it promised bliss and happiness. But of course she was not happy. She had the husk and not the substance. In London, she had thought of Italy as an island where she and Jonny would be alone. She had imagined that, without diversions, Jonny might fall in love with her, that her own love and affection for him would ignite something in his heart, that she would possess and be possessed by him. But they were not on an island by themselves. They were in the world and the world was full of attractions — like, Emma whispered ruefully to herself, Paolo Grasselli.

Her reverie was interrupted by a knock at the door. "Emma!" It was Jonny's voice. "You've been in there hours! Have you drowned?"

"I'm coming out now," Emma called, reaching out for a towel.

"The Grassellis have sent a maid over,"

Jonny said, "to ask if you want a dress pressed."

"Oh, I do!"

"Well, tell me which one and I'll give it to her."

"In my biggest suitcase, the pink cotton," Emma called out. She stepped out of the bath and wrapped the towel around her. She heard the thump of the suitcase as Jonny found it and opened it and then he called, "Okay, I've given it to her!"

When Emma emerged from the bathroom some minutes later, Jonny had gone. She wrapped her housecoat about her and walked to the edge of the balcony and looked over it.

Jonny who had obviously also bathed and changed, was busy down below moving the furniture about. He had also re-hung some of the pictures. His surroundings were very important to Jonny and Emma had to admit to herself that the way he had rearranged the room added to its comfort and appearance. He had put the couch with its faded pink cover unobtrusively against the wall which supported the gallery. At each end he had set tables, one with a reading-lamp for his own comfort and convenience.

One whole wall of the studio was practically made of glass set with a door which led on to a small terrace.

Emma watched him as he set up his easel with his back to the wide expanse of glass and light. She did not speak and he was unaware of being observed.

Oh, Jonny, Emma thought, how I love you. Even the way he moved had the power to stir her heart. He was decisive yet unhurried, lithe and graceful. In repose, as now, unanimated, his face had a brooding, almost moody look. Oh, Jonny, how I love your face, every dark, mysterious line of it, Emma thought.

A figure appeared at the door of the studio hidden by the crisp folds of her pink full-skirted frock. It was the maid carrying the newly ironed frock on a hanger in front of her.

Emma turned away from the balcony and met the girl at the top of the stairs. Emma discovered she spoke no English but she smiled her thanks.

When Emma went downstairs some time later, wearing it, her hair well brushed, her make-up fresh and light, she felt more able to cope with any problem which presented itself.

She found Jonny lying back in one of the cane chairs on the terrace studying the view. It was a pretty one with low terraced hills, in the distance, a plain of peaches in the foreground.

Geraniums and creepers grew in pots, flourished luxuriantly up the walls of the studio and spread their green tendrils over the mosaic floor.

Jonny's head turned as she came through the door. He looked her up and down lazily, but he did not remark on her appearance.

"Come and sit down," he said, not moving himself. "I've almost been asleep."

"After all your furniture moving," said Emma. "You should have waited for me and I would have helped you. It looks much better."

"I'm glad you approve," said Jonny. He spoke formally, almost stiltedly. There was a constraint between them, and Emma at the same time wanted to dispel it and wondered at it. Their relationship, at least on the surface had always been free and easy.

"Ugo Grasselli seems very kind and generous," she ventured, lighting herself a cigarette.

Jonny sat up. "A patron of the arts indeed," he said, taking the cigarette from her and putting it in his own mouth. "I suppose it is as good a way as any of spending your surplus money."

Emma, a little nonplussed by his action, lit herself another cigarette. "And what a beautiful girl Paola is," she added.

"Beautiful," Jonny said. He examined the tip of his cigarette as if he was not sure whether it was alight. "But not very paintable, you know," he went on. "Too smooth, too beautiful. I like more irregular features. Still, I must do my best by her. I think Ugo will want a portrait with character as well as beauty and likeness."

Too smooth, too beautiful. Emma thought of his words later that evening as she sat at the other side of the dining-table and watched Jonny and Paolo in animated conversation. Surely nobody could be too beautiful? Everything about Paola seemed flawless. The way her hair curled into the nape of her neck, her skin, her profile, the thick sweep of her lashes. She was very vivacious. Her eyes flashed and her teeth sparkled as she talked to Jonny. They were getting on like nobody's business. Not even mine, Emma thought. I don't have any real right to be jealous.

At dinner, Emma and Jonny had been introduced to another member of the Grasselli household. This was Elena, Paola's cousin. Elena, small and pretty, was twenty-two, and normally lived in Rome but her family was abroad travelling and so she had been spending the summer with Paola and her father. Like Paola she was tanned a beautiful golden brown. This tan she had acquired at San Carlo, a resort some 100 kilometres from Florence where the Grassellis had a seaside villa. The girls had spent all of June and July at San Carlo.

"I long to go back," sighed Elena. "San Carlo is the most beautiful place. It has a wonderful beach and the sun shines and yet it is cool especially at night."

"They are on the beach all day long, swimming, boating," said Ugo. "It is very pleasant for a short while, a good rest. I generally come up to Florence for one or two days every week, however, to see to my business."

Emma listened politely. Eventually, it dawned on her that the Grasselli family had only come to Florence partly to meet them, partly for Ugo to carry out some business, and when Mr. and Mrs. Brereton were comfortably settled in, Paola and her father and Elena were all returning to San Carlo and would not be back in Florence until September.

"You must let me make some preliminary sketches of you before you go," Jonny said to Paola. "I would like to rough out some ideas for your father."

"How long do you take over a portrait?" asked Ugo.

"Sometimes, I take a long time," said Jonny. "Other times, everything goes smoothly from the start and I can finish the thing quickly."

"After dinner," said Ugo, "Paola wants

to show you some of her own work. We will be interested to hear your opinion. I think she has a proper talent, but then I am a prejudiced father. She has been studying with one of our more famous Florentine painters but now she thinks she has come to the limit of what he can teach her."

"I should very much like to see your daughter's work," said Jonny politely without conviction.

Emma knew that it was this aspect of the Grasselli prize which had attracted him the least. He thought Ugo Grasselli was probably a fond father, blinded by affection to his daughter's shortcomings as an artist, and besides he did not like teaching.

Glancing at Ugo Grasselli's shrewd face, Emma did not think he would put too high a value on Paola's talent. His house everywhere gave ample evidence of his taste, as well as his wealth. Through the long french windows of the dining-room could be seen a glimpse of the beautiful Grasselli gardens with their tinkling fountains. The light glittering from the crystal chandeliers above their heads splintered out across the terrace to a row of cypress, jet-black against the dusky midnight blue of the sky.

The walls of the dining-room lined in crimson damask were also hung with many paintings both ancient and modern, and there were many other beautiful objects to catch the eye, urns and vases, pieces of statuary. It was all sumptuous and the long table at which they were sitting was equally so with its beautiful gold decorated china and gleaming glass goblets, with a waiting servant behind practically every chair.

After dinner, Ugo took them to an equally beautiful drawing-room and while Elena poured out coffee for them Paola disappeared and returned a few minutes later with a portfolio under her arm. She laid the portfolio on a table and did not mention it. It was Emma who, knowing Jonny would not refer to the drawings, suggested that Paola showed them her work.

Tentatively, she began passing round her sketches. There was no question about her talent, and Jonny in his newly found enthusiasm, was finally kneeling on the floor with the sketches laid out all around him.

They were nearly all drawings of people. Emma recognised sketches of Ugo, Elena, and as well there were many studies of country people, obviously estate workers and servants.

"Paola, why don't you take Mr. Brereton to see some of your oils?" Ugo Grasselli asked. "They are all round the house," he added in explanation to Emma. "I have hung quite a few and then I think Paola has some more in her room."

So they went on a little tour of the house, Ugo and Paola and Jonny clustered together, Emma and Elena bringing up the rear.

"Paola is very clever," observed Elena to Emma as they stood in front of one picture on a landing. This one was a landscape and Emma recognised the low hills which she could see from the terrace of the studio. "But then she is clever at so many things. She can embroider beautifully, and she knows a lot about music. She can play the piano and the mandolin like a dream. Last winter she had a tame music master, but that did not work out too well, did it Paola?" Her tone was teasing as she addressed this last remark to her cousin.

Paola flashed her a warning look and then glanced at her father, but he had not heard, being immersed in conversation with Jonny.

Emma was aware of a hidden meaning behind Elena's teasing reference to music but it was much later before she discovered what it was.

"That's old history," Paola whispered crossly. "You know I've always preferred painting to music."

Elena laughed. "You have many talents but you flit from one to another like a butterfly," she said a little scornfully. "You should concentrate on one and not — not spread yourself so thin!"

"Well, I am concentrating," said Paola, "on painting!"

"As you once concentrated on music!" Elena laughed again mockingly. Paola coloured up a little and turned away.

Emma pretended to be looking at the picture on the wall during this exchange, but she was interested in the little glimpse it cast upon the cousins' relationship which perhaps was not as honeyed as it seemed.

Later, Emma said curiously, almost speaking her thoughts aloud, "I know Jonny is very good and all that, but I cannot understand why Signor Grasselli does not have an Italian paint you. After all, there are some very good ones — "

Elena interrupted her, "Oh, but it is much more chic to have an English artist — my uncle likes to be different from everyone else. Besides, he dearly loved my English aunt and he is a great Anglophile. He also likes to think of himself as a patron of the arts — like a Florentine prince hundreds of years ago!"

Paola said, "Elena is always joking. I don't think you give your husband's work enough credit, Mrs. Brereton. My father loved the paintings he saw in the Warwick Galleries and even though Elena makes fun of him as a patron of the arts, he does know quite a lot about painting."

They were back in the drawing-room now and Jonny and Ugo Grasselli joined them a few minutes later.

"I probably won't be able to teach you anything," said Jonny looking at Paola, "but I will be happy to try. Would you come and sit for me to-morrow? I want to get to work straight away, and then perhaps after the sitting, you yourself could work with me? The afternoons I plan to reserve for going into Florence."

He caught hold of Emma's hand and glanced at her quickly. "Come along, Emma, it's late, and it's time for bed."

"I have a torch for you," cried Paola, "so that you can find your way through the garden."

As they walked into the cool night air, down the shadowy path which led to their new home, Jonny murmured, "Quite a successful evening. I did not think I could be so stimulated by a Sunday painter!"

"Sunday painter? But you seemed to think she was good."

"She is good," said Jonny, "but she dabbles at it. She's not got a professional approach."

"Elena said something of the sort," said Emma. "How clever of you, Jonny, to guess."

"But I am clever," Jonny said, "didn't you know?"

They had reached the studio and he let go of her hand to open the door. The big glass wall shone in the moonlight, diamond bright.

Jonny opened the door for her. "I suppose I ought really to carry you across the threshold," he said. "This is our first real night together. You couldn't count that sleepless time in the train. But there, I shouldn't make a mockery of it, should I, Emma?"

He walked into the studio and switched on some of the reading-lamps as he spoke.

Emma closed the door behind her carefully. She leaned against it, a sudden resolve in her heart.

"Jonny," she said slowly, "I wish you would stop harping on the fact that we are married, be like you were before."

Jonny turned to look at her. He spread his hands wide. "But we are married," he said, "there's no getting away from the fact. We are not as we were before. It is difficult to pretend we are. I feel this situation is very unfair on you, Emma, neither one thing nor the other."

"And probably very unfair on yourself?" Emma asked.

Jonny agreed, almost, it seemed to Emma, ruefully as though he were surprised at himself.

"I am only human," he said, "or shall I say, 'I am a man — with a man's failings.'"

And you meet someone as attractive as Paola Grasselli, thought Emma, and you feel trapped because you can do nothing about her. Jonny was clearly interested in Paola. Emma had seen his approach to so many girls before. The warm and friendly, yet provocatively detached, interest. How could Paola help but be intrigued, but of course, Jonny was married. It would cramp his style.

"You don't have to worry about me," Emma said.

"Well, if that is the way you want it," Jonny said.

"It is," Emma said. She stared at him for a moment, wondering if she had misunderstood him.

"There is no need for you to feel trapped," she said.

"Trapped?" Jonny asked. "I said nothing about being trapped. We're talking at cross purposes." Emma was still leaning against the door. "Come and sit down, Emma, and let us talk this thing out properly." He began pacing about the studio restlessly. Emma did not move. She stayed by the door watching him with bright unhappy eyes.

"Emma," Jonny said at length. "There is no getting round the fact that we are married. We did a mad thing for a mad reason. It has altered our relationship whether we wanted it to or not. We are not free any longer."

"But you said you felt free this afternoon," said Emma, "marvellously free."

"That was in a different context," said Jonny, "for the first time in my life I am free of all domestic responsibilities. All that I have to think about is painting. But in exchange I have given up another freedom. I am not one person any more. I have you to consider now."

Emma was silent, her heart beating uncontrollably.

"This evening," Jonny went on, "I

suddenly understood I was not free to follow my desires any more, to pursue any passing whim, and yet what was I to be faithful to? To whom do I owe allegiance? I find it odd of myself," he added. "I made a promise without giving what I promised a great deal of thought and yet now I find the promise holds, has power over me."

He paused in his pacing and turned round and looked at her. "I began thinking about you after dinner when we were wandering round the house looking at those paintings. A lot of women get on my nerves. You don't. You don't know much about painting but you know you don't know much. You are sympathetic to my ambitions. You are intelligent enough to keep out of my way when I want to be alone." He began pacing up and down the room again. "In fact we suit each other well enough, Emma. Our friendship is as good a basis as any for marriage — proper marriage, that is. We should share that room upstairs as man and wife. We cannot go dancing round each other like a couple of waltzing mice for a whole year. It would be too unnatural a life."

"How romantic you make marriage sound!" said Emma faintly.

"Well, marriage is not very romantic, is it?" asked Jonny. "And our situation is not very romantic, but we can make the best of it, Emma. I've racketed around long enough. It's time I settled down with a practical, sensible person like you."

"How humdrum you think me!" Emma flared in sudden uncontrollable fury. "And supposing I don't want to settle down in this arid, submissive way? What am I supposed to get out of this domestic compromise?"

Jonny seemed surprised at her anger. "You get a husband in the full sense of the word," he said. "We could lead a normal life."

Emma was silent a moment and then she burst out: "A normal life? You think other, *normal* couples start their marriage on such a basis? It's love which makes a marriage go!"

"That's romantic tosh," Jonny exclaimed. "Romantic love never lasts — it's merely a heady, blind, transient emotion!"

"It may be transient for you," Emma

cried, "because you have never really been in love!" No one, she thought bitterly, has ever touched your stony, selfish heart. "You're the most selfish person I've ever known. The person who is foremost in your mind when you put your foot out of bed in the morning is Jonny Brereton!"

"I am sorry you find me so repellent," Jonny said. He sounded both bitter and surprised. "I suppose if I had dressed up my proposal in fancy words, it might have been more acceptable to you. I have done you the honour of being honest with you. I cannot tell you that you give me butterflies in the tummy when you don't, that I shiver and shake before I meet you — " he hesitated a moment.

"However you had phrased it," Emma flashed, pride coming to her rescue, "your proposal would never have been acceptable to me."

Jonny laughed harshly and disbelievingly. "Then you must be mad to tie yourself to a man you find so very unattractive."

Emma was silent. Not mad, her heart cried out, or if mad, crazy for years, because I have loved you for years, *you* give *me* butterflies in the tummy.

"I have thought you were fond enough of me as a friend," Jonny went on silkily. "I have never thought you found me completely repulsive as a man. But now you are forcing me to believe you married me purely for mercenary reasons, for the sake of coming to Italy, for the sake of an adventurous change in your life after Elizabeth got married."

"You can believe what you like," said Emma dully, "my reasons were at least as good as yours."

Jonny flung himself down on the couch. In the shadowy dimly lit room, Emma could barely make out his expression. He was staring at her directly. The lamplight made the planes of his face look harsh and sombre. His eyes were deep pools of black.

"You present quite a challenge," he said thoughtfully, after a long silence, "but, of course, you are too young and inexperienced to be aware of it. You don't know what you are refusing. Your head is wrapped in dreams."

"My head is not wrapped in dreams," Emma snapped, her anger rising again.

"I know exactly what I am refusing — a convenient practical, physical relationship which, you think, will take away your appetite for other — forbidden — adventures. I don't want a marriage on those terms. I believe in love and being loved."

"You know," whispered Jonny softly, "I could make you eat your words, shake your belief, but don't panic, I won't even try. But, if you feel so deeply and so romantically about marriage, why did you ever marry me in the first place?"

"One reason, strange as it may seem to someone as egocentric as you," said Emma slowly, "was so that you could come to Italy and claim this prize."

"Oh, yes, of course, how altruistic of you," said Jonny, "I'm deeply grateful, Emma. Run off to your bed now, in your part of the house. You need have no fear that I will ever disturb you there. We'll stick to the bargain we made!"

As she lay in bed, sleep did not come easily to Emma. She tossed and turned, going over every word of her conversation with Jonny. She was hurt, mortified, outraged. She also wondered if she had been absurdly foolish. Supposing she had agreed to Jonny's suggestion. Perhaps half a loaf was better than no bread. Supposing she had said to him: 'I married you because I love you.' Then she would have been completely in his power. Then indeed he would have been the master, throwing her crumbs of affection when he was in the mood, more patronising, more arrogant even than he had been to-night. She could not be subjugated so completely. Her pride forbade it. She must be taken as an equal or not at all. She wanted all his heart and body or nothing.

She knew exactly what had happened to-night. He had been attracted to Paola and in the normal course of events would have pursued his interest, but he had been pulled up short by the fact that he was married. She wondered what he would do now. Miserable and muddled, she fell into a troubled sleep.

The next morning, Emma awoke early. She could hear someone moving about downstairs, and then later came the chink of china and the delicious aroma of coffee.

"Emma!" She heard Jonny call her name in a husky whisper. "Are you awake? Would you like a cup of coffee?"

In answer to her "Yes, please," he appeared at her bedside, face unshaven, his black hair ruffled, clad only in shorts. Without speaking, he put the coffee on her bedside table and flapped down the marble staircase in his sandals.

Emma threw her legs over the side of the bed and drew her housecoat around her. Her head throbbed and she felt terrible. She had a strange sick feeling somewhere deep in her heart and the memory of her conversation with Jonny the night before came flooding into her mind. In retrospect, it all seemed worse. She wondered if Jonny had been thinking about it when he had slapped down her coffee so wordlessly.

She picked up her cup and found the coffee hot and refreshing. She wandered over to the balcony and looked down. Jonny was painting, half turned away from her, slashing and plunging at the canvas with the deepest concentration.

She thought, 'He only really thinks about painting. He has probably forgotten last night.'

Between half-past eight and nine, Mario came over from the villa with fresh coffee and *brioches* and *marmalata* which to Emma's initial surprise turned out to be peach jam.

She sat on the terrace in her housecoat and ate her breakfast in the soft morning sunshine. Jonny joined her, now shaved, still wearing only shorts and sandals. He looked brisk and invigorated as though the work he had been doing had been a kind of pep-up tonic for him.

Emma leaned forward in her chair. She did not look at Jonny but she poured him out a cup of coffee and passed it to him. The sun was warm on her face, the garden smelt sweet with insects whirring away among the grass and flowers but constraint hung like a cloud in the air.

Emma said, bravely making conversation, "You were up very early. Thank you for the coffee."

"I couldn't sleep," Jonny spoke laconically, "and I wanted to work. Mario left me some coffee to warm up." She met his glance. His eyes were hard, impersonal.

"What are your plans for to-day?" he asked. "I shall work all morning, and then this afternoon I want to go into Florence. Do you want to come?"

"I should like to, if you don't think I would be in the way."

"Why should you be in the way?" asked Jonny coldly. "Don't you think you should take advantage of the opportunities now that you have got to Italy?"

"Of course," said Emma helplessly. "You misunderstand me. If you wouldn't stare at me with that disagreeable look on your face, I could explain."

"My dear Emma, I shall look at you how I choose. That is one privilege I claim as a husband and we have a whole year in which to explain ourselves to each other."

He rose from his chair as he finished speaking, looking above Emma's head at someone who had appeared at the door of the studio.

Emma turned round. It was Paola, a slender exotic figure in her tight white pants, a brilliantly patterned silk shirt and flat gold sandals.

"I hope I am not too early," she said.

"Of course not," Jonny smiled. "Let's get started."

Paola was almost as keen as Jonny on work, Emma reflected, although in the days which were to follow she wondered whether it was art which had captured Paola's attention so completely — or the artist.

This morning Paola sat, as still and tranquil as some bronze figurine while Jonny made innumerable sketches. While Emma pottered about, unpacking, washing some underwear, doing her nails, sorting out her clothes, she heard them talking. Occasionally they laughed, Jonny's husky chuckle mingling with Paola's lighter tinkle. The sound of their laughter made Emma's heart contract as though a hand had squeezed it. She and Jonny had shared so many jokes.

Later, when she had done all her chores, Emma came down into the studio and found that Paola had stopped posing as a model and had been put to work by Jonny. He had given her a still life to do and had started a canvas himself. Arranged on a cloth was a tumbling profusion of red and yellow peppers, peaches and grapes.

Elena had also walked over from the villa and now sat on the studio couch, chattering contentedly away. Plans for the afternoon had been discussed and changed. Now Paola was going to drive Jonny and Emma into Florence and Elena was also going to accompany them.

"But I am going to shop," said Elena firmly. "No Uffizi for me."

"There is only one thing," Paola added, "we must not be too late coming back. Kit Sundine is arriving this afternoon. He is driving down from Rome." She looked at Emma and added in explanation, "He is another cousin. Soon you will know all our family — "

"Impossible," interrupted Elena. "We hardly know them all ourselves."

"But Kit is special," went on Paola, ignoring her. "He is our English cousin. He is the son of our mother's brother and has been working in the film business in Rome. He will stay with us for a few

76

days and then drive down to San Carlo with us."

"He is very, very charming and attractive," said Elena. She looked at Emma. "Would you like to come for a walk before lunch? I will show you round the gardens. I know how English people love gardens."

Emma followed her into the bright sunshine. Elena led the way through the shrubbery back to the formal garden in front of the villa. Parterres of geraniums, in all the shades of red and rose, flame and pink, great banks of brilliant zinnias, flared and burnt against the sombre green of ilex and yew.

Emma, thinking about Jonny and Paola left alone in the studio, only half listened to Elena's chatter.

Elena said, "You are lucky, Emma, to have such an attractive husband."

Emma looked at her in sudden alarm. Had she been speaking her thoughts aloud? Elena went on tranquilly, "And of course he is very lucky to have you as a wife. Every time I look at Jonny, I want to laugh. It is a very private joke but I will explain. Last winter, my Uncle

Ugo engaged a music master for Paola. His name was Arturo and he and Paola fell in love. Oh, it was very exciting. I came down from Rome just when it had all been found out. There was a terrible row. Arturo was poor and not of good family. He and Paola were madly in love but it was hopeless and eventually Arturo was banished. But guess what? Your Jonny is exactly the same type, you know, dark, reckless-looking, like — like a corsair. I was very amused when I first saw him and I thought to myself, 'How very fortunate he has such a pretty wife or otherwise we would have that Arturo business all over again,' and while it was fun while it lasted, I don't think I could go through it all again. Paola is very emotional, you know. Like all artists," she added understandingly.

"Yes," said Emma dryly.

"And one must admit, very spoilt," said Elena. "Paola, I mean. Her father has always indulged her every whim. I am afraid my parents are much stricter."

# 3

**D**RIVING into Florence in the afternoon, Jonny said to Paola, "Do you know a man called Loudon Brighouse? He is a friend of my old professor and I have an introduction to him."

"I know of him," said Paola. She glanced briefly at Jonny who was sitting beside her. Elena and Emma were in the back of her little red sports car.

Paola went on, "He is an American painter who has lived in Florence for years."

"So I understand," said Jonny. "Old Maxwell Graham seemed to think I should meet him. I believe he has quite a little coterie of artists around him. I must admit I can't think of anything more dreary or boring than a lot of painters sitting around and talking about painting."

"Do you want to go and see him this afternoon?" asked Paola.

"I don't want to go and see him at all," said Jonny, "but I suppose I shall have to take up the introduction out of courtesy to old Graham. He was very keen for me to meet him. This afternoon I just want to wander round Florence and get the feel and smell of the place, but perhaps I could call in on him on our way home."

"And how long do you propose to go round feeling and smelling?" asked Elena from the back seat. "Do I have to find my own way back or can I meet you all somewhere later on?"

There was some discussion about time and place but eventually Paola and Elena came to an agreement on a rendezvous.

"I do not want to be too late back because of Kit," said Paola, "also we must not exhaust Mr. and Mrs. Brereton on their first expedition."

"Do you know I think it is time we became Jonny and Emma," Jonny said. "I am not going to go on calling you Signorina — " he paused a moment and then added deliberately, "Paola — and Elena."

There was a moment's silence and then

Elena laughed and said, "How nice of you, Jonny."

Emma noticed that Paola made no comment but she also noticed that for the rest of the afternoon Paola called Jonny, Jonny, but still addressed her as Mrs. Brereton. Emma said nothing about it. She did not even think it was deliberate. It was merely that Paola felt more at ease with Jonny. They were together in a kind of inner circle. There was sympathy between them, a rapport which did not exist between her and Paola.

I am on the outside looking in, thought Emma. I am not a creative artist, only an appreciator. But, after all, she told herself a moment later, I, the appreciator, am necessary to the creative artist.

Despite this sudden feeling of aloneness when Elena had left them, cheerfully bent on her shopping, she enjoyed Paola's guided tour. Paola was a true Florentine and knew and loved her city and as they wandered down the narrow streets, in and out of the museums stuffed to the roofs with treasures, Emma for a moment forgot her unhappiness. It returned in intermittent waves, however, as she saw

Paola's absorption with Jonny. Everything he had to say seemed very interesting to her. As it has always been for me, thought Emma sadly. How could Jonny resist those huge brown eyes fixed on his face with such concentration?

"Didn't you say you wanted to learn Italian, Mrs. Brereton?" asked Paola as they crossed the Ponte Vecchio. "Not far from here lives an old lady who would probably give you lessons. She has been teaching for years. I will show you her house and then to-morrow I will telephone her, if you like."

Emma thanked her and said yes, she did want to learn Italian. "I have also been wondering," she added, "whether you know of any Italian family who would like some English conversation. I should like to do some work while I am here. Jonny is going to be so busy and I am not going to have an awful lot to do in the studio."

"I might be able to find you someone," Paola said. "Or my father may know of a family. I will make some inquiries."

At the end of the afternoon, Emma and Paola dropped Jonny at the apartment of his professor's friend, and then went on themselves to the café where they had arranged to meet Elena. Jonny said he would join them in half an hour or so when he had paid his duty call.

Elena was not there and Emma and Paola sat in the late afternoon sunshine and ate ice-cream. Paola, apparently, had a passion for ice-cream.

'She is quite babyish in some things,' reflected Emma, looking at the beautiful dark creature the other side of the table, spooning up peach ice-cream with all the uninhibited enjoyment of a child.

"I have liked this afternoon," said Paola in her careful English. "Your husband is very stimulating. It is very nice to show Florence to someone as appreciative as you."

"You are kind to give us your time," Emma murmured conventionally.

"Your husband — Jonny — makes me feel as though I really might paint something worth while one day," Paola went on. "So often before I have got discouraged because what I plan never turns into what I produce."

Emma nodded sympathetically. However

complicated and complex Jonny's feelings might be about Paola, she thought, Paola's about Jonny were guileless and serene. She was innocence itself. It had obviously never occurred to her that her present absorption in art might be construed as absorption in the man rather than the work.

And perhaps I am nasty to think there is subconscious attraction there, Emma's mind went on. I must not be one of those women, who, because they are in love with a man, think everyone else is, too. So boring, for one thing, she added wryly to herself, spooning up her last trickle of ice-cream.

A lot of packages were suddenly tumbled on to the table. They both looked up. It was Elena.

"I have had a wonderful time," she said. "Sometimes, you know I think the clothes are almost better here than in Rome."

She ordered an ice-cream and looked about at the tourists who were now filling up the tables. For the next half-hour she amused herself by guessing nationalities.

And then Jonny appeared. Emma saw

him before the others. He turned the corner of one of the narrow streets which led into the piazza where their café was situated. For one split infinitesimal second, Emma looked at him as a stranger and into her head came the thought, much, much quicker than it takes to say, 'What a marvellous-looking man!' And in the flick of an eyelash, recognition came, and she realised it was Jonny. He is always more marvellous than I remember, she thought, watching him weave his way through the crowds on the pavement, lean, handsome, moving with a kind of animal grace. He was dressed casually in light-coloured slacks and a pale blue faded check shirt. His throat rose, a brown strong column out of the open neck of the shirt. His face was sombre, as it so often was in repose, and yet Emma sensed long before he arrived at their table that he had enjoyed his visit to the American painter.

And so it turned out. "An odd set-up," Jonny explained to her. "A kind of school and yet it isn't. There were seven or eight people there, different nationalities, and the work they are producing is quite extraordinary." His eyes glinted with a kind of suppressed excitement. "I think you would be interested." He glanced across at Paola, "And you too, Paola. The dedicated atmosphere there would do you good. I shall have to take you sometime." He explained that he had arranged to spend two afternoons a week at the studio of Loudon Brighouse. "I know it will stimulate me," he added by way of explanation.

"Will you work there?" asked Emma curiously.

"Partly work," said Jonny, "partly listen to Loudon Brighouse talk. I understand why old Graham wanted me to meet him. He is a quite fantastic person."

"I hope we all see him sometime," said Elena.

"Oh, you will, you will," Jonny said and lapsed into silence.

Driving back to the villa, he sat in the back of the car with Emma but he did not talk the whole way there.

"I shall begin to think Mr. Loudon Brighouse knocked you on the head," said Emma. Paola and Elena were chattering away in Italian in front.

Jonny closed his eyes for a moment. "I do feel as if I had been stunned," he said but did not elucidate this remark.

When they reached the villa, Elena insisted that they all came in and looked at her purchases.

She unwrapped them — a summer cotton, a beautiful embroidered skirt, some silk shirts.

Emma's eyes glistened as she looked at the bright and beautiful array. She fingered the skirt. "It's lovely," she said, "and how exquisite even the lining is. I should be tempted to wear it inside out!"

Jonny glanced at her. "Why don't you buy yourself some clothes here?" he said. "They are the most fabulous colours."

"I'm broke," said Emma simply, without thinking.

"I'm not," Jonny spoke shortly. "Why don't you make a plan with Paola — or Elena? I'm sure," he glanced at the two Italian girls, "either of them would love to show you round."

"Of course, of course," Elena and Paola chorused. "We'll go to-morrow,"

Elena said. "I love any excuse to go shopping."

Later, when Jonny and Emma were back in the studio by themselves, Jonny returned to the subject. He brought out his wallet and took out some large worn lira notes. "Here you are," he said, "for your shopping expedition."

"I don't want it, thank you," said Emma. "I spent quite a lot of money on clothes before I came — the wedding dress and so on. Besides, I don't want you to spend your money on me."

"I'll spend my money how I choose," said Jonny. "Come on, take it. In some things, I am going to have my way." He thrust the notes at her and Emma took them unwillingly.

Afterwards, when Jonny had gone to bathe and change, Emma wandered out on to the terrace of the studio.

It was early evening and the sun had set, suffusing the sky with pink and flame and duck egg blue chiffon banners. There was a bluish dust haze in the air. As she looked across the farm lands to the far hills, the scene seemed ineffably peaceful and serene, in violent contrast to her own disturbed feelings.

She stepped off the terrace into the garden. Perhaps a stroll down the gravelled paths, past the tinkling fountains, in the evening air scented with verbena and tobacco plant, perhaps a walk in such surroundings might soothe her emotion.

I am jealous, she thought, that is what all this is about. Jealous of Jonny's interest in Paola, of hers in him. How stupid she was and how destroying a feeling was jealousy. How could she help it? She felt insecure, unloved, unwanted.

Feeling her heart was a battleground, Emma wandered on, only half noticing where her steps were taking her.

The path ended in a kind of grotto, surrounded by evergreens. There was a little pool, presided over by a mossy goddess holding an urn on her shoulder. The water at her feet was covered with lilies and green weed. The lilies, pink tipped, were all closed up for the night. Emma looked down into the water and beneath the flat plates of the leaves and the green fronds of the weeds, she caught the occasional glimpse of a goldfish. She stayed by the pool for a while, letting time pass over her unnoticed. She sat down on the edge of the stone basin. It was then she noticed that at the foot of the goddess, there was an inscription carved in the stone. It seemed to be in English. Emma leant forward in an effort to decipher the worn letters.

Afterwards she never knew how it happened because it was so sudden. She felt herself slipping, tried to recover her balance, failed, and toppled backwards into the pool. As she went under, she gave a small startled shriek.

The pool was only about five feet deep and she surfaced almost immediately, with the taste of brackish water on her tongue. As she raised her arms out of the water, she saw they were covered with green slime and she could feel the slime on her hair and face.

She waded to the edge of the basin, as a man came running up the path which led to the grotto.

He leant over the basin and hauled her out. For a second, she thought he must be one of the gardeners and then he spoke and she knew he was the

English cousin whom Paola Grasselli had expected earlier.

Emma stood dripping by the side of the pool. She looked down at herself. She was covered in green slime from head to foot. Her thin cotton dress clung to her in figure-revealing folds.

Kit Sundine's eyes raked her. I must look the most terrible sketch, thought Emma, and I feel the most utter fool.

"I'm Emma Brereton," she said formally.

"How do you do?" said Kit and bowed. "I'm Kit Sundine," and then he laughed at their formality. "I'm glad you're human. For a moment, I thought you must be a water nymph — a naiad."

Emma went on helplessly, "I think I had better go and change."

"I'll come with you," Kit said. "You must be the painter's wife. I met your husband half an hour ago up at the villa."

Emma turned back along the pathway, dripping at every step. The sun had gone now and the breeze blew cold on her damp skin.

Kit Sundine walked by her side. He was friendly and solicitous. "I didn't see you fall in," he said. "I only heard you call out. You sounded very frightened."

Emma smiled ruefully. "I was very surprised," she said. "I lost my balance trying to look at the inscription. I must have astonished the goldfish." She put her hand up to her wet hair and tried to squeeze the water out of it.

The studio was empty when they arrived

"Your husband is up at the house," Kit said. "I believe you are coming to dinner — so I will see you then, Mrs. Brereton. Are you sure you are going to be all right?"

"Oh yes, thank you," Emma said quickly, anxious to be rid of him and his amused face. "I am going to have a bath and change. You probably won't recognise me when you see me again."

"I'm sure I shall," said Kit.

"I promise you I won't look quite so green," Emma said and shut the door on him.

She padded up the stairs leaving damp footprints on every step. Her dress must be ruined, she thought, looking down at it streaked and stained with the weed, and her sandals would surely fall apart when they were dry.

She ran herself a bath and stripped and put her dress and underwear to soak in a basin. How ridiculous can you be, she wondered. Momentarily, the sudden physical shock had driven her emotional problems out of her mind. By now, Kit Sundine must have got back to the house and told them what had happened to her. Jonny would surely come over and pick her up. She washed her hair and rubbed it half dry with a rough towel. By the time she had powdered and scented herself, and put on clean underwear, she felt much better.

She looked over her clothes and wondered what to wear. She hesitated over her wedding dress. It was simple and beautiful and suitable for a summer dinner but it would remind Jonny of their wedding day. And perversely, she did not want to remind Jonny of his marriage, or for him to think that she might be wearing it with such a purpose. So she left the blue dress on its hanger and wore instead one of her old cottons which she had bought last summer and which, while looking fresh and pretty enough at home, seemed, in contrast with Elena's and Paola's clothes, so uninteresting and insipid.

Her hair was still damp but she had dried it as best as she might. It was dark now and she went downstairs and switched on the lights. There was still no sign of Jonny and the misery which she had been holding so firmly at bay swept over her again. She thought 'I don't suppose he would have cared if I had drowned in that horrid slimy pool.' She might have hurt herself, caught a chill, anything. At least you would think he might come and see she was all right. She did not know, apart from Kit telling her, that they were supposed to dine with the Grassellis. The arrangement had never been discussed with her. She found herself angry as well as mortified at Jonny's cavalier treatment. She thought, 'I will stay here in the studio until he has to come and fetch me.' She paced about the room for another ten minutes. It was nearly eight o'clock. Did she achieve anything by being childish? Perhaps it would be better to hide her anger, to remain bland, and walk over to the villa as though it were a perfectly ordinary thing to be abandoned like this? Emma suddenly decided she could not bear for Paola Grasselli to know one detail of the relationship between herself and Jonny. She picked up her handbag and the torch which Paola had given them.

When she arrived at the villa, the servant Mario took her to the terrace at the back of the house. There she found Paola and Elena, Kit and Jonny lying in comfortable chairs, enjoying long cold drinks tinkling with ice. Lights from the house shone across the terrace. As well, for illumination, there were candles set in tall iron sconces protected from the breeze by glass chimneys. Paola had taken her portable gramophone on to the terrace and was playing some of her favourite records and the music was soft in the background.

For a moment, Emma stood in the doorway. It was a charming scene, like a stage setting. Beyond the soft flickering lights of the candles, the garden was dark and mysterious, and farther beyond still, through the trees could be seen the twinkling lights of the village.

As they became aware of Emma, Jonny and Kit rose from their chairs, and Paola also came forward to greet her.

"What an age you've been!" Jonny said and then added, "I hear you've been paddling!"

"Paddling?" Emma repeated after him, trying to control her voice. "I had a complete ducking. I've been cleaning myself up."

"The naiad," Kit Sundine said. "I recognise you perfectly, Mrs. Brereton." He turned to Jonny. "I have never seen anything so pretty or so composed as your wife rising out of that pool. I really thought she was the statue come to life. And then she introduced herself and I knew she was no water nymph but an English lady."

Emma gave a little uncertain laugh. He was teasing her but his friendliness warmed her heart after Jonny's indifference. "I must have looked extraordinary," she said.

"I am so sorry," Paola said. "I don't think anyone has ever fallen in before."

Emma explained again how she had

been so stupid and after some more teasing and laughter, the subject was dropped.

Ugo Grasselli was not at home for dinner and there were just the five of them. In a little while, Paola suggested they had dinner.

Emma found herself sitting next to Kit, opposite Jonny who was between Elena and Paola.

In her confusion by the pool, she had not looked at him properly or even noticed exactly what he was like at all. Now she became aware of him as a personality. He was good looking in a tough sunburned way, with very blue eyes. He was gay and laughed a lot, showing strong white teeth. He was teasing and affectionate with both Elena and Paola as though they were funny children.

As she began the fried *scampi* which made the first course of their dinner, Emma said politely, making conversation: "I believe you are in the film business in Rome?"

"I've been working there for a few months," Kit said. Looking at him speculatively, Emma asked, "Are you an actor?"

"God forbid," Kit's tones were fervent.

"But you are working in a film?"

Kit nodded. "You must have heard of the film. It's an enormous spectacle of the Roman Empire at the height of its power. Lots of chariots and chariot races. I'm in charge of the horses. I'm a horse-breeder by profession. Or at least my father is. We have some stables just outside Newmarket."

"And how long will the film take?"

"Well, it's taken longer than it should so far. I was supposed to be out here six months but it will be next year before I go home, I should think. We had trouble collecting the horses. They were too expensive to buy in Italy as at first planned so I had to go over to Yugoslavia to buy some and then get them shipped over here and since then we've been training them."

"It sounds exciting," said Emma.

"It is," Kit said, his eyes on her. "Some of the chariot races have been pretty good. You'll have to come to Rome and see some of them."

"I should like to," Emma said.

"And what do you do?" asked Kit. "Do you paint too?"

Emma shook her head. "I have no talents," she said lightly

"Except for looking decorative and delicious, wet or dry," said Kit.

"Thank you," said Emma. She glanced across the table at Jonny but he was absorbed in an argument or discussion with Paola and Elena. The two girls were talking across him very quickly and vehemently and suddenly both of them broke into Italian, their English not being up to whatever it was they wanted to express.

Kit raised his eyes to heaven. "My mad Italian cousins," he murmured.

Jonny held up his hands between the two girls. "Be quiet," he said, laughing. "Speak in English!"

Elena suddenly shrugged and laughed but Paola fell back in her chair with a sulky pout to her lips.

"What are they fighting about now?" asked Kit goodhumouredly.

"We were discussing Italian actresses who go to Hollywood and make good,"

Jonny said. "Elena and Paola don't have the same opinion on any."

"They have the same opinion on nothing," Kit said.

There was a lull between courses and a lull in the conversation.

"Does anybody mind if I smoke?" asked Kit. He turned to Emma. "Would you have one, Mrs. Brereton? Or don't you own to such a barbaric habit as smoking between courses?"

"Thank you," Emma said, stretching out a hand. Kit passed his case across the table to the others and then bent forward and lit Emma's cigarette for her. Emma gave him a quick upward glance and then looked down again. Her eyes were a smoky blue and thickly lashed. They were beautiful and the most striking feature of her calm little face. She was unaware of their beauty — although she accepted they were nice enough — and she was also unaware that the look in them was sometimes more provocative than she felt.

"Please call me Emma," she said.

The words, plus the swiftly veiled look, caused Kit to look at her with surprise and a warmer interest in his eyes.

"Okay, Emma," he said lightly. "Although you don't look like an Emma."

"My mother was a Jane Austen fan," Emma said. "What does an Emma look like?"

"Prim and proper."

"What about Emma, Lady Hamilton?" asked Jonny, from the other side of the table, interrupting their conversation.

"Aha I had forgotten about that charmer," said Kit. "Are you a *femme fatale*, Emma?"

Emma looked across at Jonny. I know one man who doesn't think so, she wanted to say, who considers me about as glamorous as a peahen. Jonny met her glance, his eyes hard and mocking. Emma laughed a little defiantly. "Doesn't every *femme* want to be *fatale*?" she said. She flashed a smile at Kit.

Jonny leaned across the table. "No," he said deliberately. "There are plenty of women, thank God, who don't want to be *fatale* at all, who don't want to be Cleopatra or Madame de Pompadour — who just want to be their honest, straightforward selves . . . "

"Oh dear, so serious!" said Emma faintly. "I was only making a joke!"

"Who wants to be Cleopatra?" cried Elena. "I would rather be Lollobrigida — or — or Princess Margaret!"

"Not Lollobrigida," Paola said.

They began arguing again about films and the conversation became general.

After dinner, they went outside again on to the terrace to have their coffee. Their chairs were in a rough circle round a low marble-topped table on which the coffee cups were arranged.

"Why don't you sing to us?" Kit suggested to Paola. "It is just the evening for it."

"Didn't you know?" asked Elena. "Paola never plays her mandolin now — all her attention is given to art."

"Do you play the mandolin?" asked Jonny with interest. He was sitting the other side of the table from Emma and his face was in shadow, but now he sat up and his face came into the light.

"Oh, I used to," Paola shrugged, "but I got tired of it. I haven't played for ages."

"It's such a pretty tinkling instrument,

do play for us, Paola," Jonny said.

After a little more persuasion from Kit, Paola got up and went into the house and then came back a few moments later with the instrument.

Jonny, with his characteristically concentrated air, examined it. "Such a decorative shape," he murmured, smoothing his hand over the deeply rounded body, which was inlaid with mother-of-pearl flowers and leaves. Through the curved hole in the centre below the strings, he read out the label, *F. del Perugia, San Piero a Ponti, Firenze, Anno 1926.*

"My mother used to play it," Paola explained, taking it from him. "I shall be very rusty. You must excuse me."

She began tuning it, and in a little while hesitantly tried a lilting tune, accompanying it in a soft low voice.

It was enchanting. Emma lay back in her chair and Jonny did likewise. The sound died away and nobody moved or spoke for a second or two. It was as though Paola had cast a spell on them all.

"That was beautiful," Jonny said, and Emma's heart stirred at the warmth and admiration in his voice.

"Beautiful," she echoed after him, meaning it. Paola's voice had been exquisite and she clearly had not lost her skill with the mandolin.

"I told you she was good," Kit said complacently. "Sing some more, Paola." He rattled off the names in Italian of some songs he liked, and Paola, after strumming for a bit, paused and then began again. Her voice floated out into the shadowy garden, soft and sweet and compelling, the Italian vowels as pretty as bird song.

The terrace, half in light, half in shadow, the cool night air, the flowery scent of the garden beyond them all seemed part of the texture of Paola's music. She was singing a love song, a sad unfulfilled love song, nostalgic with plaintive longing.

Above the trees the stars were beginning to come out. Emma, sad and troubled as she was, felt caught up in a web. As they all were, she thought, glancing round at the group, lying, relaxed, in their chairs, not moving, not stirring, except for Kit as he smoked his cigarette. The tip of it glowed red in the shadows beside her. How could Jonny not be bemused with Paola who had so many talents and so many facets to her personality?

Paola's voice trailed away into silence. There were one or two more sad lost notes from the mandolin and they too died away.

Somebody sighed, perhaps Elena, perhaps Emma. The long drawn-out whisper of it seemed to stress the tangible emotion in the air, as though Paola had conjured up spirits of long-lost loves, of enduring loves still to be.

Paola put down her mandolin and stood up and walked over to the coffee table. "The coffee is cold," she said and broke her own spell. "Does anybody want any more? Or anything else to drink?"

Even at the end she is clever, thought Emma, leaving them all not sated but wanting more.

"Nothing for me," Kit said yawning. "It's time I hit the sack. I've had a tiring day."

"Oh, don't go to bed yet," protested Elena. "What are our plans for to-morrow?"

"Well, it's work for me and for Jonny," said Paola quickly. She turned to Emma. "Would you like me to take you shopping in the afternoon?"

"I shall also be going into Florence again," Jonny said.

They made tentative plans and then said good night.

Jonny and Emma did not speak as they walked back through the trees to the studio. Jonny walked a little ahead shining his torch on the sandy path.

He opened the studio door and motioned her inside and then followed her in and switched on all the lamps.

"Are we going to have dinner every night with the Grassellis?" asked Emma suddenly. She stopped halfway to the stairs which led to her bedroom.

"I shouldn't think so," said Jonny, peering at the canvas on his easel. "Why do you ask? Have you a sudden desire to go all domestic and start cooking?"

Emma did not answer. In her imagination, before they had come to Italy, she had seen herself preparing meals for Jonny, for just the two of them, having the fun of marketing in a strange place, running their home, but this she would not admit out loud.

"Oh, I am sure nothing I cooked would be as elegant or delicious as the Grasselli's," she said coldly.

Jonny scratched at his canvas with his nail. "Oh, you're a good enough cook," he said. "I shan't worry if we have to depend on you, but there is rather a poky little kitchen back there. Anyway, the villa will be empty soon. We must find out what arrangements are to be made about us."

Emma's heart felt suddenly lighter. Of course, Paola would be gone soon. In another five or six days she would return to San Carlo and then she and Jonny would really be on their own.

"If I'm not going to have any household duties at all," Emma went on, "I'm not going to have much to do."

Jonny turned and faced her. "You'll have your English and Italian lessons," he said. "What's the matter with you?"

"Nothing," said Emma. "But I should also like to be told when we are expected to dinner at the villa. I didn't know we were supposed to be going there to-night."

"I am sure I told you," Jonny said, "you certainly were very late."

"That was because I fell in the pool," said Emma nettled.

Jonny said, "You walked into the garden without a word while I was changing. I didn't know where you had gone. I presumed you had gone over to the villa before me. I didn't know you intended to fall in the pool."

"Oh!" Emma cried crossly. "I didn't intend — "

"Well, at any rate, Sir Galahad came to the rescue," went on Jonny.

"He was very kind," said Emma stiffly.

"Evidently," Jonny said. "Don't think I didn't notice him making goo-goo eyes at you, and you encouraging him by flapping those great long eyelashes of yours at him," he added. "You'll be giving him ideas about yourself, which I'm sure you wouldn't want to." He stared at her mockingly. "One thing I can't stand," he said mock sententiously, "is a man who runs after a married woman."

"You are absurd," Emma said a little breathlessly. How dare Jonny say things like that to her when he paid court to Paola in so blatant a manner! He really was impossible. "Good night," she said and turned on her heel.

Long after she was in bed, and had turned off her light, Jonny was still awake. Emma could see the reflection of his lamp on the high raftered ceiling of the studio. He must be reading. She herself could not settle to read, neither could she sleep. She thought how odd and sad and ironic it was that he should lie there in his part of the house and here she was in hers, wakeful and restless.

A barrier was growing — had grown — up between them, a barrier which had not been there before they were married.

# 4

EMMA and Paola went shopping in the late afternoon when the after lunch somnolence had disappeared from the streets and *boutiques*. Emma spent the money Jonny had given her with reckless abandon. She knew she was spending with a purpose, to impress Jonny, to give every aid to herself to compete with Paola. And yet even as she did it, she knew it was pointless. Jonny was interested in clothes, critical or admiring as the case might be, and he had decided views on what suited her. But clothes never made a man fall in love with you. But, of course, they could make a man notice you. Sometimes, Emma thought, that was what the matter was with Jonny and herself. She had been around too long. There was nothing surprising or intriguing about her. She was not a mysterious new girl who had suddenly appeared on the horizon, with all the allure of a *princesse lointaine*. She wished she could create a new Emma.

She did her best with her purchases. They were unlike any clothes she had ever bought before. It was as though the Italian air had given her a new daring, a new nerve to wear something she would never have tried under the eagle and fastidious eye of her very fashion-conscious sister, or the benevolent gaze of the head at the prep school. As she stared at herself in the mirror, trying on a scarlet linen, form-fitting sheath, embroidered with sprays of black and green, Emma for a second thought of the school where she had spent two years as a secretary. For a moment in her nostrils, there was the ghost of that special school odour, composed of furniture polish and ink, chalk and dust and the emanation given off by small boys. It all seemed a million light years away.

"That is very chic," cried Paola enthusiastically, bringing her back to the present. "It suits you. Very good for your figure."

Emma bought the scarlet sheath, and then another yellow silk frock, high waisted with a stiffened, bellshaped skirt, and little cap sleeves attached to a deeply curved neckline. She bought tapered slacks in white and purple, flat gold sandals, a big straw handbag, a wide pink straw sun hat. She bought presents too, a straw bag for her sister, a stole for Jonny's mother. She also bought herself some dazzling silk blouses of exotic colours and designs.

She felt much better when she had finished but also slightly breathless. She had never bought so many things at one time in her life before. Always she had planned her clothes purchases so carefully, never buying on impulse, always trying to stick to her budget. Perhaps she would hate all the things the next day but looking at her parcels, somehow she did not think she would.

They were in their last shop of all, a little shop tucked away in a narrow street, which sold beautiful skirts of velvet and taffeta ribbon. Paola wanted to order herself a skirt to be made for the winter. Emma did not think she should spend any more money although she still had a few thousand lira left. While Paola looked at patterns and models, she fingered some of the skirts absentmindedly.

Then a friend of Paola's came into the shop. They greeted each other with ecstatic cries of welcome, and Paola introduced Emma to the young woman who apparently was not long married and who had just returned to Florence from her honeymoon. Politely, for Emma's benefit, they spoke in English for a moment or two, and then lapsed into their own tongue.

Emma wandered off, smiling vaguely. Everything sounded so exciting and excited in Italian. Paola and her friend were probably only discussing the clothes in Paris, but they sounded as though they were exchanging secrets of violent and disturbing importance.

A salesgirl accosted her, holding out a gold and crimson skirt, indicating it would fit Emma. Emma shook her head although she eyed the skirt longingly. But it was madness, where on earth would she wear it?

Paola joined her. She was flushed and smiling and apologised for keeping her waiting. "I will come back another time for my skirt," she said. She tossed a few words at the salesgirl and then added to Emma: "Let us go and have an ice-cream. I know a very nice café where we can go."

Emma did not feel very much like an ice-cream, but she agreed out of politeness.

Paola set off down the narrow street shadowy in the evening light.

They crossed a piazza where horse-drawn carriages waited in line for customers, the coachmen dozing on the boxes or gossiping with each other by their horses' heads. Paola turned down another street and then another, finding her way unerringly, and after about five minutes walking, they came to the special café. They had passed many other cafés on the way, their checkered tablecloths and gay little plastic chairs set invitingly on the pavement and in the roadway under awnings, interspersed with tubs of flowers and shrubs. Twice, Emma, tired, had suggested that they stop and have their ice-cream at one of them.

But Paola said, "Oh, but the Caravella is much nicer. You'll see. It is worth going there. It is a chic place."

When they finally reached it, to Emma it did not seem much different from any of the others. It was in one corner of a piazza, set with an ancient fountain in the middle where pigeons roosted. The Caravella had rows of little tables set out on the pavement outside. The umbrellas which shielded the tables in the daytime from the sun were now sheathed. Tubs of flowers were set as outposts round the tables. Behind in the café-bar itself, there was a small dance floor and a piano at which a man was sitting and tinkling out a popular tune of the moment which was relayed through a loudspeaker to the customers in the open air.

Emma and Paola sat down and disposed their parcels about them. Paola gave their order to the waiter and then looked about her. Her eyes were very bright as her glance darted about inquisitively. She looked across Emma's head into the café, across the small dance floor and saw the young man at the piano. She looked away again quickly and Emma wondered why she seemed so excited.

Their ice-creams were brought and Paola had a quick conversation with the waiter. Emma was bemused thinking of her purchases. She ate her ice-cream without really paying much attention to Paola's agitation. It was only when a dark young man was standing at their table, looking down at them, that she began to guess why exactly they had had to come to the Caravella.

She became aware that the loudspeaker was no longer tinkling piano music over their heads.

"Oh, Emma," said Paola, "may I introduce a friend of mine, Signor Valli?" The young man and Emma bowed at one another. "Can you sit with us for a moment?" asked Paola.

Signor Valli cast a look across his shoulder and spoke in Italian.

Emma guessed that he was saying he must get back to his piano. He and Paola had a little more hurried conversation and then he bowed at Emma again and was gone. A few more minutes and the music began seeping out again.

"He couldn't stop," explained Paola and then added unnecessarily: "He doesn't speak very much English."

Later, as they were walking to the

square where they had parked the car, she said in an off-hand manner, "I would be happier if you did not say anything to my family about Signor Valli. He is an old friend but you know how it is — he is only playing in the café for the holidays — he is still studying — but my father is *très snob* as the French say."

It was only then that Emma began to remember Elena's story of the music master, and to wonder if Signor Valli's first name was Arturo. But she felt it would be prying to ask. After all, it was none of her business. She began to wonder if Paola was as guileless as she seemed.

She also wondered if she should tell Jonny about the encounter and knew, as she thought about it, that her motives for telling Jonny would not be altogether pure. But perhaps Jonny should be warned off Paola, and then she thought, no, Jonny must look out for himself. She remembered that Elena had said Jonny reminded her of Arturo: "Dark, reckless looking." Signor Valli was certainly dark and good looking enough, but he was nothing like Jonny. He was a fairly ordinary looking young man.

"I have made an appointment for you to meet Signorina Chierichetti," said Paola, breaking into her thoughts. "I thought we could call and see her on the way home, and you could make arrangements about your Italian lessons."

Emma had her first Italian lesson the next morning. She went into Florence by herself. Feeling adventurous, she walked into the village, caught the bus and found her own way back to Signorina Chierichetti's apartment in the heart of the city. She was glad to get out of the Grasselli studio, to get away from the villa and all its inhabitants. She longed to get her brain working on something concrete again.

Jonny was full of energy, on what Emma called one of his working jags. She had seen him in this mood before, remote, preoccupied. If she hadn't thought it sounded corny, she would have said he was inspired — by the light, the Italian sun, the landscape around him, perhaps by Paola. Besides working on Paola's portrait, he had started two other canvases.

118

This morning he had been up at seven again, working like someone possessed. As before he had brought her up a cup of coffee. She had barely been awake when she saw him standing by her bed and he had vanished before she had properly opened her eyes.

And Paola was in the studio, to pose, to paint, before Emma was dressed. Jonny's enthusiasm seemed to have infected her in equal strength.

"Oh, yes," Elena had said last night, "Paola is a great enthusiast. Now it is nothing but paint, paint, paint, Jonny, Jonny, Jonny, and work, work, work. This summer she will paint all the time but I would like to bet that at the end of it she will put her brushes down and not pick them up again for years."

Emma, looking across the drawing-room where Paola was talking with a group of her father's guests and Jonny, wished she would put her brushes down right away.

Last night Ugo Grasselli had given a dinner party, as a prelude to his leaving for San Carlo. About twenty of his friends and friends of Paola had driven in from the countryside around and from Florence.

Memories of the party occupied Emma's thoughts as she sat in the bus on her way to Signorina Chierichetti. It had been a grand and formal evening. Emma had worn her new red dress. She had felt nervous but also quite pleased with her reflection as she walked down the stairs from her bedroom.

Jonny was waiting in the studio below. He had stared at her as she came down the stairs, in a hard and appraising way which had made the blood come to her cheeks. All he said, however, was, "You've done your hair differently!"

Normally, Emma kept her hair pinned back above her ears with two combs. Now, to-night, she had let it fall free on either side of her face.

"Do you like it?" she asked involuntarily.

"So-so. It makes you look different," had been Jonny's answer to that.

Yet later, she had heard him compliment Paola on her dress and also Elena in warm and admiring words.

Emma looked at the countryside rolling past the bus windows. She might as well face it. She was not a type Jonny admired. But then what was his type? Looking back on all his girl friends, they had no common denominator except looks of a very high order and a certain something one might characterise as dash, and dash was something you were born with. The Dash Fairy, along with all the others, wasn't at my christening either, thought Emma dolefully. And then she addressed herself sternly and sharply and said, "Enough of this self pity!"

Kit Sundine had admired the red dress, but somehow Emma felt he had paid her a compliment to make her feel better. She had been standing alone at the beginning of the party, feeling shy and a little out of it, and he had come up to her and hummed a snatch of song, "Oh, the lady in red . . . all the fellows are crazy for the lady in red . . . " and then he added: "How pretty you look, Emma!" and, very skilfully, he had drawn her in among the guests.

Many of Ugo Grasselli's guests spoke English as well as he did, but they were talking Italian among themselves. They broke off when Kit introduced Emma.

With Kit by her side, Emma did not feel so shy and essayed a little stilted small talk. As soon as Kit saw she was launched, he moved unobtrusively away. He was, in fact, a much better host than Paola was a hostess. She was intent on enjoying herself and left her guests to look after themselves. Most of them, indeed, knew each other very well, and Paola saw to it that they very soon knew Jonny. She took him round the room with her, introducing him not only as the Grasselli prize winner but also as her *maestro*. Emma somehow was not included in this little tour. Admittedly she hung back, not wanting to trail after Jonny as some dull domestic appendage and it was while she was hesitating in the doorway that Kit came over and rescued her.

Later she saw him do the same for an Italian guest who also seemed to have got stranded with no one to talk to. She was a young girl devoid of make-up. It did not make Emma feel any better to notice how very plain she was. Not all Italians were as beautiful as Paola, she reflected, or even as beautiful as the peasant women she now saw washing in the communal laundry as the bus careered through a village.

It had been an illuminating evening. Even people you knew well appeared different when they were in a crowd. She had got a new perspective on Kit. He had paid her flattering attention ever since he had arrived at the Grasselli villa. Now she saw it was his social manner. He treated all the girls, even the plain ones, as though they were queens. She had been pleased by Kit's interest but she did not feel chagrined to notice that he seemed equally interested in all the other girls. He had a warm and friendly nature and watching him smile and laugh and flatter, she felt it was a warning not to take his interest too seriously. Not that she had been in any real danger of doing so, but she had to admit that at times, after Jonny's attitude, Kit's attention to her had been a solace.

Jonny himself had been a big success at the party. He had not been madly gay like Kit, but his brooding good looks, and the praise Paola had heaped upon him, had caught the notice of most of the men and all of the women there. After dinner, he had been dragged into some game of chance Paola had arranged at the other end of the drawing-room. While Emma talked, she was conscious all the time of the laughter and shouts which were coming from that end of the room.

Once, Kit, seeing her eyes wander to the roulette table said, "Let us go and see what's going on!" They had stood behind Jonny's chair and watched for a little while. Jonny had turned round and asked Emma, "Do you want to come and play?" She had shaken her head and Kit, bored, said, "Come and get some fresh air," and had taken her on to the terrace. For some reason, Emma had been conscious of Jonny's eyes on her as she left the room and she had turned at the door to see if he really was staring, and had received from him a most extraordinary, piercing look. A little shaken by its intensity, Emma joined Kit by the balustrade. Kit was smoking, looking out into the garden.

He said, "Something tells me you're not very happy, Emma. I imagine life with a temperamental artist is not easy."

Caught off balance, Emma had been silent for a moment and then she had replied, "Jonny's not temperamental and I'm perfectly happy." Her tone was cold and snubbing and Kit was quick to apologise.

"I shouldn't have said that, should I? But you must look happier, Emma, if I'm to believe you."

"I just have a naturally miserable face," Emma had said, with a forced laugh.

"What rubbish. You have a very gay little face." He sighed and added, "I am very glad you — and, of course, Jonny — are here. I am very fond of my Italian uncle and my mad Italian cousins but they are a little exhausting sometimes. I shall be able to catch your eye and know that you are thinking exactly what I am thinking!"

"You won't have many more days to catch my eye," Emma had replied. "When do you go to San Carlo?"

"Oh, there's some talk of our staying longer," Kit had answered idly. "Uncle Ugo and Elena will go, of course. Elena longs to be back on the beach, but Paola wants to get on with her painting, and your husband, I believe, has produced some marvellous studies which have pleased my uncle very much. He thinks the portrait proper should be begun at once, and of course Paola must be here for that."

"Oh, yes," said Emma quietly. Her heart had sunk at his words. That island on which she and Jonny alone were to be marooned was fading rapidly out of sight.

"And what about yourself?" she had asked.

"There are as many attractions here for me as there are at San Carlo," Kit had said looking at her. But Emma heard no personal implication behind his words.

"Yes, it's very pleasant here," she said mechanically.

Kit put his hand on her shoulder. "More than pleasant, I think," he said.

It was then that Jonny had interrupted them. He stood at her elbow and said, "Time to go home, Emma."

Nothing more had been mentioned about San Carlo, and this morning, Emma, as she got out of the bus and looked about in Florence, felt more buoyant. Kit had probably only been talking idly. Paola as well as Elena was longing to get back to San Carlo. If she and Jonny could be alone together, for even just a few weeks, Emma felt she could get their relationship back on to an even keel again and that this strange feeling of antagonism between them would disappear.

# 5

SIGNORINA CHIERICHETTI'S apartment was at the top of a large old-fashioned building. Emma managed to find her way there without mishap.

The signorina was small and dumpy and fierce and her methods of teaching seemed old-fashioned to Emma. By the time she left the dark cluttered little apartment, she felt about nine years old again.

Under her arm, she carried the text book the signorina had provided and an exercise book of rules and her homework book.

After the coolness of the Chierichetti apartment and the hall and stairs of the building, the sun in the street seemed strong. Emma walked along, planning to get a taxi as soon as she came to a rank.

She had another appointment. True to her word, Paola had made inquiries and

128

last night Emma had been introduced to a youngish couple who had teen-age children and who told her they would very much like her to have lunch at their house once or twice a week and give them conversation in English.

Emma felt shy and a little nervous at the thought of her lunch, but she was also glad that she had got the job. It meant a little extra money so that she would not be too dependent on Jonny, and it also meant an extra interest to her days.

Signor and Signora Campanelli had seemed a pleasant and interesting couple.

The Campanellis lived on the outskirts of the city in a large villa surrounded by gardens, and Emma's pupils turned out to be Cataneo who was known as Ciccio, a twelve-year-old boy, and seventeen-year-old Julita and fifteen-year-old Bianca.

At that first lunch everyone was shy and not much conversation took place, and Emma was relieved when it was all over and she was on her way back to Florence again. Signora Campanelli drove her back in the family car.

"Next time it will be better, I hope,"

Emma said apologetically.

"Oh, I am sure it will," the other woman replied pleasantly. "They know quite a lot of English, you know, but their accents are very bad. We will look forward to seeing you again."

She dropped Emma at the café where Jonny had said he would meet her. But there was no Jonny waiting for her. Instead, Kit Sundine rose lazily from his chair at an outside table as she approached.

"Hallo," he said. "Jonny was sorry but he wanted to go on working. I came in to pick you up."

Emma was disappointed not to see Jonny because she had hoped that they might have a wander round together but she also understood that if he were in the middle of something which was going well, he would not want to disturb himself, so she smiled and said, "It is very nice of you to come for me. I hope I have not been a nuisance."

"No nuisance at all," said Kit politely. "Do you want a drink or an ice-cream or anything?"

"I have only just finished lunch,"

said Emma, glancing at her watch. She grimaced slightly when she saw the time, a quarter to four.

"It must have been a very long lunch," said Kit. "How did it go? Was your conversation sparkling and idiomatic?"

"Oh, very," said Emma, ruefully thinking of the long pauses while she manœuvred her spaghetti and racked her brains for something to say. The Campanelli children had stared at her politely but owlishly from three pairs of large liquid dark brown eyes. Ciccio had been the friendliest and the most promising.

"Do you want to go back to the villa right away?" asked Kit. "I have some shopping I want to do, and I thought this might be an opportunity."

"Oh, please do your shopping," said Emma politely. "I am in no hurry."

"Well, that's fine," Kit said briskly. He signalled to the waiter and paid his bill.

He turned round and took Emma's arm, and they threaded their way across the piazza through the traffic into one of the narrow lanes.

"I want to buy myself some shirts,"

Kit said easily, "and Paola a birthday present. It is her birthday next week."

"But she will be in San Carlo," said Emma involuntarily.

Kit glanced down at her, "But she's not going," he said. "I thought I told you last night."

"I didn't know it was definite," Emma managed to answer. They were walking in shadow now and the lane in front of them seemed dark and black after the brightness of the sunshine in the square. Emma felt sick with chagrin. So Paola was going to be around all the time, posing, painting, taking them on tours of Florence. She could have cried with exasperation and frustration.

Kit was talking, "Ugo and Elena are leaving on Friday," he said, "driving down. But I am staying up here with Paola. She says she's too absorbed in what your husband is teaching her to want to leave. They settled it all this morning, while you were at your Italian lesson. Your husband has started on the portrait of Paola, I understand, and he feels it would also be a pity to break off now."

"Yes," said Emma, "I had a peep of the canvas yesterday."

Jonny and Ugo had finally decided on a pose for Paola between them. Jonny was painting her on the terrace of the villa. She had her back to the garden and part of the garden with its trees and blue skies could be seen in the background.

"And what about you?" asked Emma. "Painting is not keeping you here too?" she tried to smile up at him and her face ached with the effort of it.

"No," said Kit, "but I didn't particularly want to go to the beach. I am content enough to loll around here. Also there is the *palio*, the horse race in Siena the week after next, and I want to go and see it. I have never yet managed to get to it, and I thought it would be simpler to drive over from Florence than all the way from San Carlo."

"What is the *palio*?" asked Emma mechanically. She did not believe Paola was staying in Florence because of her painting. It was because of Jonny. She was fascinated by him.

"It's a medieval horse race which takes place in the main square of Siena," explained Kit. "It's very romantic and elaborate I believe. I'll take you with me. That day we'll leave the painters to get on with their painting." He stopped outside a man's outfitter's. "Here is my shirt shop. Do you want to come inside and help me choose?"

Emma followed him inside. Now Jonny and Paola would be thrown together constantly. No one would think it odd or unreasonable. She wondered what they were doing right this minute, and with a sudden heart-rending flash, she realised that she did not trust Jonny. How could she love a man she did not trust? But she did, and that was all there was to it. How wild and fantastic had been her dreams about this marriage! "What do you think of this blue stuff?" Kit interrupted her thoughts. "Or do you think the stripes are more dashing?"

"They are all very nice," said Emma.

"Oh, come Emma, you must give it more of your attention than that! Choosing shirts is a very serious business," Kit said jokingly. He was having his shirts made to measure and was now only selecting the silk.

Emma shook herself mentally. She must pay more attention to Kit, who was being so particularly nice to her. She must not be so ill-mannered. For the rest of their shopping tour, she pushed the image of Jonny successfully from her mind, but a kind of hobgoblin of misery settled on her chest, or her shoulder, a black lump which seemed as tangible as a growth.

After he had settled the problem of his shirts, Kit turned to Paola's birthday present. They wandered from little fashion shop to little fashion shop, looking at scarves and belts, gloves and bags. In the end, he decided on a silk scarf. While he was completing his purchase, Emma's eye had been caught by a display of costume jewellery. A bracelet of iridescent pink beads tempted her and she took it in her hand and looked at it more closely. Each translucent little bead was gold tipped and the chain they were suspended on was also gold. It was very pretty.

"Do you like that?" asked Kit. "Let me buy it for your birthday."

"But my birthday is several months

back," said Emma.

"I'm so sorry," said Kit, "I always forget about dates. Let me give you this belatedly. You look as if you want cheering up somehow. Were your two lessons so very grim?"

Emma's eyes filled with unwelcome tears. Kit stared at her.

"I didn't mean to make you cry," he said. He took the bracelet from her and handed it to the salesgirl to be wrapped up.

"You mustn't — I can't — " protested Emma. But Kit would not listen to her and a few minutes later thrust the tissue-wrapped gift into her hand. Emma felt slightly uncomfortable about the gift but did not see how she could go on refusing it without seeming churlish. She glanced once more at the jewellery counter and wondered if she should buy Paola a present for her birthday. And then she decided against it. It seemed a little obtrusive and unnecessary. Perhaps the day itself they could mark with flowers, she and Jonny, unless Jonny of course preferred otherwise.

When Emma arrived back at the studio,

neither Jonny nor Paola was there. Elena came over from the villa with a message. They had gone into Florence after all.

"Jonny said he wanted to go and see Loudon Brighouse again," said Elena, "and so Paola drove him in. We tried to think of some way of reaching you so that you could all meet. But of course it was impossible. How did your lessons go? Can you speak Italian yet?"

"Not till I've done my homework," said Emma as lightly as she could.

When Elena had gone, she sat down at the table in the studio and tried to learn some Italian vocabulary, and in the lined book which had been provided by Signorina Chierichetti, she started her homework exercise.

It was here about an hour later that Jonny found her.

She saw his shadow through the glass and looked up as he came in. He was humming a song which was popular that summer and which Emma had heard played in the cafés constantly in Florence. But he stopped when he saw her.

"Oh, hallo," he said.

"Hallo," said Emma.

Jonny moved towards her, hands in pockets. "How did your day go?" he asked. He stood looking down at her.

"All right," Emma said, closing up her books. "How did yours?"

Jonny leant over and picked up the exercise book and leaved through it.

"I did some rather good work," he said, "and then Paola and I drove into Florence. We tried to get hold of Kit so that we could meet you but he had gone. We went and saw Loudon Brighouse."

"Paola went too?" asked Emma quietly.

"She was dying to meet him," said Jonny carelessly, "so I took her along. I don't know whether she will join his class or not. They were not terribly *simpatico*."

Emma was silent. She had longed to meet this American who had struck such sudden strange power over Jonny, and she had hoped that Jonny would take her when next they went into the town. But he had taken Paola instead. Now nothing would ever make her ask Jonny to take her. She raised her chin proudly and took the exercise book away from Jonny.

"That's my homework," she said briskly. "I hope it's all correct or I am sure I will get caned to-morrow."

"What's this?" Jonny picked up the little tissue bundle from the table where Emma had dropped it on first coming in.

"It's a present from Kit," Emma said a little defiantly. "He bought it while he was getting a present for Paola. It's her birthday soon."

Jonny unwrapped the bracelet and held it for a moment in his hand moving it so that it caught the light, and then, without comment, he tossed it back on to the table. Looking at his face, which was inscrutable enough in expression, Emma yet had the strange feeling that he was displeased, and she felt glad. She picked up the bracelet and slipped it round her wrist. "Isn't it pretty?" she said. She slipped the catch to and held out her arm, the bracelet dangling at her wrist.

"Uh-huh," Jonny murmured and turned away. "Do you want to see the portrait?"

"Oh, yes," Emma said, moving eagerly from the table.

"I've nearly finished the 'Fruit Girl'

also," said Jonny. The 'Fruit Girl' was the name he had given another canvas he had also been working on. "Come and look at it."

The 'Fruit Girl' was a long narrow canvas. Standing to one side was a brown girl, unnaturally elongated, her nakedness partially veiled with a bright scarf. On her head was an enormous shallow basket full of fruit, and there was more fruit rolling on the sandy ground at her bare feet. Behind her were the terraced slopes which Emma could see from the studio window, the peach and cypress trees, the blue sky. The girl's face was turned slightly to the left. She reminded Emma of someone but she could not quite place who. It was a fantasy of a painting, a dream of summer; the girl was not a mortal but some dryad of the earth and trees. Yet despite the myth-like quality of the painting, there was also an intense realism about it. It glittered with heat, the sky was a brazen blue and you knew that if you picked up one of the peaches in the basket and bit into its warm sunripened flesh, the juice would squirt out prodigally and full of sweetness. Emma had been fascinated by the painting from its inception. Now she looked at it for a long time and turned away in the end with a little sigh of contentment. She did not think she could bear Jonny to part with that one. The 'Fruit Girl' was a canvas she would want to keep.

She went over to the other easel where Jonny was standing and staring at his portrait of Paola. This was only blocked in, and Paola's shape stared like a ghost from the canvas against the darker background which would eventually be the trees and greenness of the garden. And yet misty as it was, it was yet Paola's ghost and no one else's. Already there was some faint stirring of personality, of likeness in the shape of her.

"You are working well," Emma said.

"Yes," said Jonny simply, "I'm quite pleased this evening."

He stared at her a moment as though about to say something else. Emma met his glance bravely, her eyes as cold as his own. He was never going to know how hurt she was, how mortified that he had taken Paola and not her to see Brighouse.

Somehow she was going to cope with this thing by herself.

Jonny's gaze held her for a long, long moment. Emma felt there were fire crackers going off in the air around them, electric sparks of antagonism, of a battle of wills. For a fleeting unhappy instant, she thought, 'Why, Jonny really looks as though he dislikes me! What have I done? Except perhaps exist — and get in his way!'

She willed herself to turn away and did so at last and moved towards the staircase and her bedroom.

Jonny said softly, with almost a menace in his voice, "You've changed, Emma. I have never seen anyone change so quickly. You even look different. Why do you do your hair that way?" he paused a moment: "Or is it I who have changed? Perhaps Italy has affected us both."

"Perhaps," Emma said from the stairs. "Could you tell me what the plans are for this evening?"

"The Grassellis are dining out," Jonny said, "and Paola has arranged for our food to be sent over here to the studio, so you don't have to bother to dress.

Wear your dressing-gown." It sounded like an order.

Emma went up the stairs. I am still the same, she wanted to cry. She wondered why Jonny was so angry with her, but in her heart of hearts she knew the truth. She remembered the proposition he had made their first night in the studio. Indelibly every word of it was written on her heart. She had turned him down. She had affronted his manhood and his pride and the hurt still smouldered. He must have known all these years about her obsession about him. He had probably thought she was ready to fall in his arms at a word. And so she was, but only for the sake of true love. Perhaps she was very stupid.

# 6

WITH the departure of Ugo Grasselli and Elena at the end of the week as arranged, a kind of brooding quiet settled over the villa and the studio. The inhabitants of both fell into a steady routine.

Nearly every morning Emma went into Florence for her Italian lesson. Most mornings she caught the bus though sometimes she was driven in by Kit or Paola. She had a quick ear and she had application. She slogged away at her Italian, hoping by concentrating on it to take away some of the pressure of her emotions.

She left Jonny and Paola in the studio, though sometimes Paola, like Kit, slept late and apparently did not turn up till noon long after she had gone. This on occasion made Jonny angry when he wanted to get on with her portrait. Jonny was working harder than ever. He had plenty of incentive. The night before he left, Ugo Grasselli had promised him that he would do his best to get him a show in Rome in the autumn. Jonny wanted to have a good selection of canvases ready.

In the afternoons, Jonny frequently went into Florence, to study with his American friend Brighouse, or to contemplate the many, many treasures of the city. Sometimes he and Paola went to Brighouse together. Sometimes Emma met them afterwards and Kit joined them for an apéritif at one of the bars or cafés.

In a way all four of them led separate existences. We are like balls on a billiard-table, thought Emma. We bump into each other on occasion or drop into pockets of our own, or all congregate at one end of the table. If it had not been for the tension between herself and Jonny and her distress at the growing warmth of the friendship between Jonny and Paola, she would have enjoyed the effortless swing of the days.

She had come to terms with Signorina Chierichetti. Her methods might be old-fashioned but they worked. Emma's Italian was becoming quite fluent. She had made friends with the Campanelli children and her twice-weekly luncheons with them were amusing and gay and gave her a window on to another aspect of Italian life.

Most evenings the four of them had dinner together, either lazily, in the studio, brought over from the villa's kitchen by Mario, or more formally in the Grasselli dining-room.

The day before Paola's birthday, Emma said to Jonny, "Do you want to buy Paola a present?"

"No. Why should I?" Jonny snapped. He was working, slashing great gobs of colour on his canvas in a kind of demoniac fury. Working something out of his system, Emma thought.

"It's her birthday," said Emma.

"I leave the giving of presents to Kit Sundine," said Jonny, glancing at her. Self-consciously Emma looked down at the pink bracelet which Kit had given her and which she was wearing to-day and did indeed wear very often, it seemed to go so well with many of her frocks.

"Oh, well, I suppose it doesn't matter," Emma said, "but I think she is having a

146

special little dinner party — just us — but an extra special menu."

"Buy some flowers if you must," said Jonny. He stared at the big palette table in front of his easel and then squirted out a great mass of oily liquid brilliant stuff from one of his tubes. He drew his finger across the paint, oblivious of the scarlet smear on his forefinger. "I love this stuff," he said dreamily. There was the warmth and passion in his voice that some men reserve for women, thought Emma. Oh, she knew well enough that not only Paola was her rival, but somehow it was easier to cope with *paint*.

In the end, in the morning, Emma walked down into the village and bought Paola a big bunch of carnations to mark her birthday. It seemed a little silly when the villa garden was so full of flowers but she felt that she and Jonny had to make some gesture. Her own mixed feelings apart, there was no doubt that the Grassellis had been much kinder and more hospitable than they need have been, well beyond the bounds of the Margaret Grasselli prize.

Paola had ordered a special dinner for her birthday and they ate it formally in the dining-room, with branched silver candelabra sending a soft glow over the table.

Emma wore the blue frock in which she had been married. It was the first time since their wedding day that she had put it on and as she looked at her blue reflection in the mirror, her heart was full of strange sadness and yearning. She felt that two entirely different girls had worn this frock. A whole ocean of feeling separated them.

The frock though was as pretty as ever. Emma was now palely tanned from walking so much in the sun, down to the village in the mornings to catch the bus, from sitting and sun-bathing gently on the studio terrace. The skin of her face and arms was a pale gold, which the blue of the dress set off to perfection, and her hair now had many bleached high-lights. Her eyes were bright and she looked well. Regular, unhurried meals, lots of rest and the sun had been a tonic to her. If I looked how I felt, Emma thought, I would be wan and pale and hollow-eyed. Instead she looked the very picture of bouncing health without a care in the world.

Later, as the four of them were sitting round the beautiful dining-table, she thought, what a handsome picture they all made, the men good looking in their different ways, she herself who looked as nice as she ever could and Paola who looked especially beautiful in a dress of apricot.

There was a curious kind of infectious excitement in the air. They laughed a lot and their eyes flashed at one another. In the close proximity of the last ten days, they had learnt to know each other very well. They made gentle fun of each other and they had private jokes. Yet it was a curious kind of spurious intimacy. I know nothing of what goes on inside Paola's head, reflected Emma, or Kit's and they know nothing of mine. As for Jonny, though she knew and understood him so well, he too had his mysterious and secret life.

Often during the meal when she looked up she found his eyes on her. In the gentle light of the candles it was difficult to make out their expression, but it seemed watchful, wary. Kit, too, stared at her a lot, boldly, without subterfuge, but it was easier to understand his look. His eyes were full of a flirtatious admiration, and Emma found herself responding to it, being gayer, more provocative than she felt or really wanted to be. She had had an odd feeling about Kit the last few days. Did he feel sorry for her that she was thrown so much on her own while her husband was so busy — in various ways — and apparently legitimately — with Paola?

Since their first shopping expedition, they had often been alone together. Kit sought her out. He obviously enjoyed her company and she enjoyed his, genuinely, on its own merits and also because when she was with him, she did not have time to brood about Jonny and Paola.

After dinner, they sat on the terrace and drank their coffee, listening to records on Paola's gramophone, and then Kit suddenly pulled Emma to her feet and said, "Let's dance." Emma found he was a reasonably good dancer and they moved up and down the terrace watched by the other two. When the music stopped he gave her hand an intimate squeeze and whispered, "That was nice." With the new tune on the turn-table, Jonny got up and asked Paola to dance, and the four of them, Kit and Emma, Paola and Jonny, went on dancing for several records more. And then they changed partners, and Emma danced with her husband.

"Do you know this is the first time we have ever danced together?" Jonny whispered to her.

"Yes," Emma murmured back. The same thought had occurred to her. Somehow in London, dancing did not figure much in their lives. Certainly she had never been to a dance where Jonny was also a guest, and when Elizabeth gave parties, she never wanted the gramophone played because she said it interfered with conversation and made too much noise anyway.

Now Emma found Jonny was a good dancer. They did some tricky steps together and when the music stopped, he laughed a little huskily and said in surprise, "Why, you're good!" He did not let go of her but kept his arm round her waist until Paola had set a new pile of records on the turn-table, and then they moved off again down the terrace, the light streaming out from the house behind them casting grotesque shadows.

Emma was stirred by Jonny's closeness. She longed to put her face near his. But that was weakness. Jonny would not be thrilled by her touch. What had he said? 'I can't say you give me butterflies in the tummy when you don't . . .'

"Why are you sighing?" asked Jonny.

"Was I sighing?" murmured Emma.

"Like a grampus," said Jonny, abruptly releasing her. "I think it's time we said good night."

Emma was tired too. The nervous gaiety of the early part of the evening had left her, and she felt deflated. They walked home in silence and after quickly murmured good nights went to their beds in silence. Jonny's light was off before hers.

In her dream, Jonny was chasing Emma down a long marble corridor. She wore high-heeled shoes and they clicked furiously on the marble floor, and Jonny himself was wearing enormous boots which made a terrible noise, and then they were suddenly, in the mysterious way of dreams, in Jonny's flat in London, and Paola Grasselli was there and she was picking up all Jonny's wonderful records and throwing them against the murals on the walls and they crashed on to the marble floors with a horrific sound.

Emma awoke. Above her head there was a crashing and rolling as though ten million barrels were being pushed around. It was thunder, and then a sudden jag of lightning flashed in through the window and lit up the room like daylight. Emma cowered beneath her sheets. All her life she had been scared of thunderstorms and this surely was the granddaddy of them all. She knew her panic was irrational but nothing and no one had ever been able to persuade her out of it. She lay trembling, waiting for the noise to subside, but, instead, it gained in fury. The centre of the storm was not yet overhead. It was approaching and it was going to get worse before it got better. She could hear the trees outside soughing as they swayed in the wind, and the loud splashing of the rain.

Wide awake, Emma lay still under the sheet. She wondered if Jonny were awake and while she was wondering, in between the crashing and rumbling of the thunder, she heard Jonny calling her name.

"Emma, get up and come down! Emma!"

Emma lay quiet and did not answer. She heard Jonny's voice come nearer. He was obviously shouting up at her from the foot of the stairs.

"Emma, don't be absurd! I know you're scared. Come on down, you silly girl!"

Emma got up out of bed and drew her dressing-gown around her and went downstairs.

Jonny had switched on a table-lamp. He was sitting on his couch, hair tousled, his face still creased with sleep. "Come and sit down," he said, as Emma appeared, and pushed aside his blanket and made room for her on the couch.

Jonny knew too much about her. That she was afraid of thunderstorms was one thing among many.

He switched off the light and they sat in darkness, lit at intervals by the flash of the lightning.

"If we had some water and a kettle we could make some tea if we had some tea," said Emma. Her teeth chattered involuntarily.

"You're a silly goose," Jonny said contemptuously. "Why are you so scared of thunder? Do you think big bogies are going to drop out of the sky?"

"No," said Emma uncertainly, "I think the roof is going to blow off and I'm going to be whipped up into the centre of the whirlwind. I don't know what I think . . . I just know I don't like thunder."

"It's very primitive of you," Jonny said, his tone still scornful and unsympathetic.

Emma felt a little wave of resentment wash over her. She thought, 'He gives and then he takes away.' It had been kind of him to call her down because he knew of her fear, and now she was here, he was doing his best to make her feel like a child and a ninny. He had been sweet and gentle for a moment on the terrace this evening and had then followed it by brusqueness. His cavalier treatment of her of the past ten days, his neglect, the leaving to her own resources, little pictures passed through her mind as she sat there in the darkness, and her resentment simmered into rage. He took a great deal of advantage of her good nature.

"You're really a baby, aren't you, Emma," he said, breaking into her reverie and catching hold of her hand. "It's something I should remember." He had moved closer to her as he spoke.

Emma pulled her hand away and leaned back, as though to avoid him.

She heard Jonny's husky laugh. "Don't shy away from me like that," he said, but there was no laughter in his voice. "I've told you before I won't bite you. Or even try to kiss you." He paused a moment. "Though I dare say it might be an interesting experiment. Some of your prudish reservations would melt away."

"I'm not prudish," said Emma fiercely.

"Well, your romantic notions then, your innocent ideas — or whatever euphemistic term you prefer," Jonny went on smoothly.

He locked his hands behind his head

and stretched his legs out in front of him and then yawned loudly.

"I've been kissed before without losing my head," said Emma angrily. "I'm not such a baby as you like to make out."

"Have you now?" Jonny said with mock interest. "You must tell me about your great loves. Four o'clock in the morning is always a great time for confidences."

"You're impossible!" Emma said. She would have liked to have stood up and run away upstairs to her bed but a sudden, extra loud clap of thunder changed her mind about that.

"Would you like some coffee? I have some ready for breakfast," said Jonny.

"Coffee? In the middle of the night? We would never get to sleep again!"

"I have a better idea," Jonny said. He got up and switched on the light again and went and rummaged in a chest at the other side of the room. "I bought some of those sweets this morning in the ice-cream shop." He found what he was looking for and walked back to the couch. He stood for a moment looking down at her. "Did I ever tell you that you are very pretty?" he said softly.

Emma meeting the dark glance felt herself flushing. Involuntarily, she put her hand up to her hair.

"Don't worry about your hair," Jonny went on in the same soft tone. "I like you tousled. You look very wild and gipsyish." He dropped the bag of sweets in her lap and then flopped beside her again on the couch. Emma did not move and Jonny said nothing more for a moment, and then he leant over and switched off the light again.

"It's nicer in the dark," he said. "Give me a sweet, Emma."

Emma silently passed him back the bag. "Don't you want one?" he asked.

"No, thank you." Emma felt she would have choked on a sweet. She felt breathless as if she had been running. Her rage of a few moments ago had simmered down again, but she was full of a desperate frustration. Why was Jonny tantalising her so? She felt he was playing with her as a cat with a mouse, and in a moment he would pounce and she would be helpless.

Jonny ate his sweet and then another and then began talking calmly, as though completely unaware of any strain in the atmosphere.

"I hope Ugo likes Paola's portrait," he said. "Before he went he promised me he would arrange a show in Rome in the autumn if I did enough canvases, and he said he would let me exhibit the portrait. If that is a success, he said, he can guarantee me more commissions. I would be the fashion."

"And of course," said Emma speaking with difficulty, "if you are the fashion in Rome, you will become the fashion in London."

She was glad that Jonny had got on to the subject of his work, had abandoned his teasing game with her, but also in a funny perverse way, she was disappointed. "There is nothing like a foreign cachet for an artist!" she added.

"Don't be so shrewd," Jonny said. "It doesn't suit you." He went on after a moment, "I took 'The Fruit Girl' into Florence yesterday to show Brighouse. He was impressed, even more so when Paola told him who the model was."

"And who is the model?" asked Emma faintly.

She felt Jonny stir beside in the darkness. His face turned towards her, a white blur.

"You, of course," he said in surprise. "Surely you can recognise your own face when you see it!"

"It reminded me of someone," Emma said, remembering the beautiful half-naked girl of the picture, "but I haven't got those long legs . . . " she faltered.

"Oh, I admit I had to use my imagination a little," Jonny went on cheerfully, "I haven't had the privilege of seeing you wearing so little, but I think Brighouse thought I had painted from life. 'Your wife must be very beautiful,' he said."

It was much quieter now. Thunder rolled in the distance far away. The lightning flashed only occasionally. The storm had passed. The rain still pattered down. They could hear it among the trees which surrounded the villa and garden.

Emma felt she could not bear this conversation any longer. Jonny was mocking her. Mocking the stand she had taken, her deeply held beliefs. He was deliberately, calculatingly shaking her foundations.

Emma got up from the couch and walked across the studio and opened the door which led on to the terrace. She stood for a moment feeling the damp air on her face, smelling the sweet fresh smell of the wet earth and vegetation. Jonny came and stood beside her. They did not speak. She could feel his eyes on her face but would not look at him. For a terrified moment she thought he was going to kiss her, and knew that if he did, she would be lost indeed, and he would have won his game.

"Good night, Emma," Jonny said, "you don't have to be afraid any more. The storm's over."

★ ★ ★

In the morning, the rain had stopped but the sky was still clouded and overcast.

Jonny and Emma, for the first time, had their breakfast inside. "But I thought the sun shone all the time in Italy," cried Emma. "Surely we're not going to have a cloudy day?"

161

Jonny grunted. He held out his cup for more coffee. He was still unshaved and looked morose and uncommunicative. He looks wild and gipsyish this morning, Emma thought, remembering his remark of the night before. She remembered his compliments as well as the unkind things he had said.

She gave him his second cup of coffee and met his glance with assurance. She had been scared last night. Before she capitulated, she wanted complete capitulation from him, but she knew now in the dull light of this rainy day that he was aware of her as a woman at last. He had been trying to provoke her, needling her to show her emotions. As she busied herself about her morning chores, she felt cheerful and for the first time since they had been in Italy, she allowed herself to hope a little.

Paola arrived for her sitting before she had finished dressing. Paola looked tired and there were heavy circles under her eyes. She complained that she hadn't been able to sleep. The storm had woken her up.

"It did us too," Jonny said, "nobody

could have slept through it."

"Kit did," Paola shrugged, "or so he told me this morning."

Emma slipped her straw handbag over her arm and picked up her books. She was going off for her Italian lesson.

Jonny looked at her, his eyes raking her from her head to her toes, boldly, almost possessively, Emma thought, as though she had appeared for his delectation and approval.

"Is that another new dress?" he asked.

"You've seen it before," Emma said nervously. She opened the door on to the terrace. "I am having lunch with the Campanellis. Is anyone coming into Florence this afternoon?"

"I'm not," said Paola yawning, "I'm too tired. I shan't even work. I shall go to bed."

"I'm not sure," Jonny said. "I shall make up my mind later."

"All right," Emma said, "then I will come back by bus. I don't expect I will be here before five or so. Good-bye." She raised her hand in a kind of salute and, without looking at either of them again, walked out of the studio and across the terrace and down the woodland path.

Sitting in the bus on her way into town, Emma was amazed at her feeling of elation. By now with her frequent trips she knew the bus driver and several of the regular passengers who always travelled at the same time. She received and gave back smiles and good mornings. Her Italian now was fluent enough for her to pass the time of day. Everyone this morning seemed as gay as herself. And the damp countryside under the cloudy sky looked, she thought, more beautiful than ever. She exchanged remarks about the storm, the sort of remarks which country people make all over the world, and then in a little while they had reached the piazza where she disembarked, and then walked the rest of the way to Signorina Chierichetti's flat.

Her lesson finished at noon and she then went to the Campanellis. There, however, a surprise awaited her. All the Campanellis were out and were evidently not expecting her. The servant who admitted her said that the arrangement had been changed. The signora had written to the signorina. He himself had posted the letter. The family had gone away for a couple of weeks, but then they would be coming back, and then they hoped the signorina would come back.

Emma realised the letter must have got delayed. Probably it had contained payment for her and she hoped that it had not got lost altogether, but it was no good worrying about it. Walking away from the Campanelli house, she debated what to do.

She would have lunch in Florence and then perhaps mooch around a bit on her own. There was so much she had not yet seen.

She had lunch at the Caravella. As usual there were plenty of English tourists and she got into conversation with an English family who recognised her as English.

"Although we weren't absolutely sure," said one of the girls in the party. "Your clothes looked Italian."

"They are," Emma smiled. "I'm trying to melt into my background. I read once that the *tourist* always looks his nationality and demands his native dishes, while the *traveller* is always taken for an inhabitant and lives on the country. I'm trying to be a traveller."

"Well, we're certainly living on the country," went on her companion, "I hate to think what all the *pasta* has done to my waistline. It'll have to be *basta* with the *pasta* from now on!"

Emma laughed. She looked around for the pianist but Signor Valli was nowhere to be seen and the piano inside the café-bar was shuttered and silent.

She visited an old church which had caught her attention before and then sometime in the middle of the afternoon went back to the Grasselli villa on the bus.

She felt sleepy suddenly and thought longingly of her bed. How pleasant a little afternoon nap would be. She and Jonny had lost several hours sleep last night. She wondered if he too were suddenly feeling the effect of the storm.

The sky had cleared now and the sun was shining brightly. The atmosphere was hot and sticky. It would be lovely to take off all her clothes and lie down in her cool room.

As she walked down the lane, already

dusty again, from the village, Emma's thoughts also turned to the pleasure of a long cold drink.

The Grasselli villa, shuttered against the sun, looked somnolent as she walked up the driveway. She turned off into the grateful shade of the wood and soon was standing outside the studio.

Afterwards she never knew what premonition, what presage of disaster caused her to pause a moment on the terrace and look into the studio through the big windows. So often in the past she had slipped across the terrace under the shade of the awning which was always down in the afternoon, opened the door quickly and was up the stairs in a flash. Emma nearly always moved quickly and Jonny was always asking, 'What's the rush? Where's the fire?'

But to-day she paused and looked in. The studio was dim and shadowy. The awning of the terrace cast a shade and the windows in the other wall were also shuttered. The light was aqueous and filtered, but it was perfectly easy to see anyone who was in the studio.

For a moment, Emma thought there

was no one, that the place like the villa was empty, and then she saw Jonny and Paola, and her heart seemed to stop beating and roll somewhere.

Jonny and Paola were standing in the middle of the room, Jonny with his back to her. His dark head was bent over Paola and her arms were entwined round his neck. They were kissing passionately.

For a split second, Emma stood there immobilised and then energy seemed to pour into her limbs as though she had been rocketed into space. She turned and fled back into the wood, down the path and down the driveway of the villa as though the demons of hell were after her.

# 7

EMMA ran without knowing where she was running but some instinct made her avoid the village with its two shops, its café, its inquisitive inhabitants who at this time of the day would be sitting in the shade and taking it easy, and watching the world go by. Instead she turned at the end of the driveway towards the countryside, running along the dusty lane until she came to a dirt track which led into an olive grove and here in the shade of the trees she finally came to a stop, too chokingly breathless to run any more.

She sat down on the dry brownish turf beneath the trees and put her head in her hands. She felt literally sick, with emotion, with breathlessness brought by her crazed running. Seared into her memory was the picture of those two dark heads so close, so confidingly together. Of course, she had returned unexpectedly early. They must have thought they would be safe for many hours more. They must have spent many afternoons in such intimacy while she was away in Florence. Oh, Jonny, Jonny, she muttered to herself, how could you do this to me? She felt her love turning to hatred inside her. She felt that if Jonny were to appear before her now, she would kill him, take revenge for the wasted years when she had so admired and loved him. She had loved someone who had never existed. She had loved Jonny's noble exterior and had given him a heart to match it. She had always made excuses for him. He was brilliant, a creative artist. He was clever. Therefore he must be allowed his moods, his egocentricities, his selfishness.

She had thought he was a man of honour. She had believed him when he had said, "I made a promise without giving what I promised a great deal of thought and yet now I find the promise holds." That was all a lot of nonsense. And last night, she had dared to hope. She had thought that he had become aware of her at last, as a woman, but as a woman of spirit, one to be considered and respected. But it had all been a game. He had been amusing himself, relieving the boredom of the thunderstorm.

As for Paola, what had he told her? That they were not properly married? Emma writhed inwardly at the thought. She had taken pride in presenting Jonny to the world as her husband. A false pride but nonetheless, unadmirable though it may be, it was there. She would not have believed that Jonny would humiliate her so.

Emma lay back on the grass and looked up into the grey-green leaves of the olive trees. It was very quiet in the grove. There were no birds, and the grey twisted trunks looked like the illustrations of a forest in a fairy story. They stretched all around her ghostly, motionless.

Emma was dry-eyed. She could not cry though she felt that if she did it might give some release to the terrible pent-up feelings she had. She felt as though her head or her heart was about to burst, and yet as she lay there, she also blamed herself for her unhappiness. She should never have come to Italy. She should never have suggested that Jonny marry her. What was she going to do now? What was Jonny going to do? How deeply did he feel about Paola? Well, she supposed she would soon know. Obviously, they would not be able to keep their love to themselves for long, and if Paola knew and believed the relationship between Jonny and herself, clearly she would know that his freedom was not an impossibility. But perhaps Jonny was not in love with Paola, merely infatuated, transiently attracted. Emma sat up and pushed her hands through her hair. That somehow made it worse and reduced the whole situation to something cheap and nasty. Emma lost count of time. She became aware at last that the air beneath the olive trees was grey and dusky and she could tell by the golden light on the hillside and the long shadows that it was getting late. She must pull herself together and go back to the studio and face whatever had to be faced.

With an unconsciously gallant gesture she threw back her head and stood up, and began smoothing the grass and twigs off the skirt of her yellow dress. She walked out of the olive grove back on to the dirt track and then into the country road, more slowly than she had come there, but her steps were resolute even if her heart was as dark and heavy and stony as basalt.

When she got back to the studio, it was empty. But as she looked round at the white walls which had suddenly become hateful to her, she sensed that people had only just left the room. It was as though the air was still stirred by the waft of their departure. There was the scent of tobacco, the sweet smell of the Italian cigarettes both Paola and Jonny smoked.

She noticed that the ash-tray on the marble coffee table was full of cigarette stubs, some of them stained with lipstick. They had evidently not spent all their time making love.

On one of Jonny's easels was the portrait of Paola. It was very recognisably Paola now. Jonny was working fast. The eyes, the mouth, the modelling of the face, all were alive and accurate. The mouth, with a slight quirk at the corners, was particularly fine. It looked as though Jonny had been concentrating on it. In more ways than one, thought Emma bitterly.

She turned to the picture of 'The Fruit Girl' which was on the other easel which Jonny used. Now that she knew she was the model, she could see herself in it although she had never known she had such a waif-like air. She had been flattered when Jonny had told her it was herself. But of course it meant nothing. How silly she had been to be so pleased about it.

Mechanically she picked up the dirty ash-tray and went and emptied it. She came back and plumped up the cushions on the couch, rearranged the chairs. Jonny was supposed to keep his painting things at one end of the room but he seemed to be spreading and encroaching on the bed-sitting-room half. Still, this was his part of the house and she supposed he could do what he liked.

She was standing indecisively in the middle of the room wondering whether she should go upstairs when there was a step on the terrace outside and the object of her thoughts appeared in the doorway.

"Well, hallo there!" he cried in a loud

cheerful voice at the sight of her. "What time did you get back? I was sure we would be on the same bus." He flung the bundle of sketches he was carrying on to the table. "I've just been up to the house to collect these. I thought I might need them." 'These' were all studies he had made of Paola for Ugo Grasselli.

He was standing right in front of her, his eyes very bright and bold as he looked down at her.

"Bus?" Emma said stupidly.

"I spent the afternoon in Florence," Jonny said.

"And Paola?" she asked.

"Oh, I don't know what Paola did. Went to bed, I think. Said she was tired." Jonny spoke carelessly, indifferently.

So this was how it was to be, thought Emma miserably. Lies, subterfuge, dissimulation, deceit. She longed to shout at Jonny. To tell him he was a liar, that she had seen him that afternoon with Paola. But she knew that if she did, she would burst into floods of uncontrollable tears and her chagrin and her mortification would be plain for him to see.

Some trace of her emotion must have appeared on her face for Jonny suddenly put out his hand and touched her gently under her chin. He tilted her head back so that her face was more in the light.

"What's the matter, Emma darling?" he asked, "you look very wild all of a sudden."

Emma jerked her chin away. She felt she could not bear him to touch her. She made as if to move away from him but he caught hold of her by the arms.

"What's the matter, Emma?"

"Nothing's the matter!" Emma said fiercely, struggling to free herself.

"It's no use struggling," Jonny said softly. "You'll never get away from me — unless I let you! Tell me what's the matter!"

"Take your hands off me!" Emma cried. At the look on her face, the ice in her voice, Jonny's eyes flickered as though she had suddenly slapped him. He released her immediately. Emma fell back a step and rubbed her arms where he had held her.

Jonny moved away, turning his back

on her, feeling in his pockets for his cigarettes.

"I'm sorry," he said over his shoulder, "to be so offensive. Keep your troubles to yourself if you want to."

"May I come in?" They both, startled, looked at the doorway.

Paola, a dark shadow against the light, stood there for a moment and then walked into the room.

Emma wondered if she had seen or heard anything of their scene.

"I've had a very good idea," Paola said, seemingly unaware of any strain in the atmosphere or if she were, ignoring it. "Why don't we go into Florence to-night for dinner?"

"I'd rather not, thank you," said Jonny shortly.

"Oh, Jonny," Paola said cajolingly, "let's do something gay!"

"I don't feel gay," Jonny said.

"Oh, but I do," Paola cried, "marvellously gay. I want to celebrate!"

Emma switched on the lamp by the side of the couch and sat down.

"What do you want to celebrate?" she asked evenly.

Paola waved her arms in the air. "Being me," she cried. "Being alive!" She paused a moment, "If you don't want to go out to dinner, can we have supper in the studio? I will ask Mario to bring it over."

"If you like," Jonny said. He did not sound over-enthusiastic.

Emma did not think she had ever had such an unhappy evening in all her life before. At the beginning of the evening, she tried to talk, to smile, as the four of them sat in the studio, their supper plates on their laps. But in the end, the effort proved too much for her and she lapsed into silence. Neither of the men seemed to notice. All their attention was taken up by Paola, who was like a fire-fly, dazzling with her brilliance. She looked beautiful and her talk sparkled so that Jonny and Kit were in constant laughter at her remarks. She is mad with power, Emma thought, noting the by-play among the three of them with a heavy heart. Jonny ignored her completely. He had eyes and ears only for Paola. She might not have existed.

Kit sometimes tried to draw her into

their charmed circle and she tried to respond but then his attention wandered and he was listening to Paola again.

At the end of the evening Kit said, "I am going into Siena to-morrow to watch the *palio*. Does anyone want to come? What about you, Emma?"

"I should love to," Emma spoke fervently. How wonderful it would be to get away for a day, to fresh surroundings, to a new scene to take her mind off her situation.

"I'd like to see Siena," Jonny said thoughtfully. He looked across at Emma for the first time that evening.

"Why don't we all go?" asked Paola. "You would enjoy the *palio*, Jonny — and Emma too, of course," she added. "It is full of colour — and excitement. We'll start off early in the morning and have our lunch there."

They did not in the end start off so early in the morning, for which Emma was thankful. She had lain awake for a long time in the night and had then fallen into a troubled sleep at dawn and in consequence overslept. But apparently everyone, including Jonny, had overslept as well. It was mid-morning before they were all dressed and ready to drive to Siena.

It was Kit's idea that they took two cars, his and Paola's. "I know Jonny is going to want to sightsee after the race," he said, "and I won't. I shall want to come home. If we have two cars, we'll be more mobile."

They were standing in the driveway of the villa while he spoke. Paola's own red sports car was drawn up a few yards away.

Paola looked at him doubtfully. "I suppose that is a good idea. I would like to show Jonny and Emma round Siena."

"You don't have to bother," said Emma quickly.

"It is no bother," Paola seemed surprised at Emma's tone. "How shall we go? Jonny and Emma will come with me?"

"And I'll be all alone?" Kit said in mock ruefulness.

Emma slipped her hand through his arm. "I'll drive with you," she said. "I'll keep you company, and the two *artists*"

— she gave the word a faintly mocking intonation — "can talk about art and not bore us." She glanced at Jonny and met a look from his dark eyes, an unkind look. She thought bitterly, "Well, let them be together. What do I care?" and yet she knew as she thought it, that she did care and that perversely by suggesting they should ride together had twisted a knife in her own heart.

Kit's Jaguar was in a garage round the back of the house and she followed him as the other two climbed into Paola's car and swooshed off down the drive.

Siena is an ancient city in the very heart of Tuscany. It is perched on the top of three hills and is divided into seventeen districts called *contrade*. Since medieval times, there has always been great rivalry between the different *contrada* and the horse race, the *palio* which they were going to see, was an expression of this rivalry.

So Kit explained to Emma as they drove through the beautiful Tuscan countryside, through the plains of peaches, through the vineyards and olive groves, up and down the rolling hills. "I've never seen it," Kit said, "but I believe it's a pretty tough race and the costumes are supposed to be marvellous, all velvet and brocade and medieval." He turned his eyes from the road and glanced at her and laughed.

"You're looking very gorgeous this morning," he said.

"Am I?" Emma said automatically. "Thank you." She was used to Kit now, and his compliments. They were the oil he used for the wheels of conversation. He liked girls and she was one of the girls he liked. He had probably been flattered that she had chosen to ride with him.

"How long have you been married?" he asked suddenly.

"Not very long."

"How long?"

"Oh, about — about a year," Emma floundered. She did not want to say that they had got married just for the sake of the Grasselli prize.

Kit was silent for a few minutes giving all his attention to driving but he had evidently been turning something over in his mind.

"You don't want to pay too much attention to Paola," he said at length.

"I don't know what you mean," Emma said.

"Oh, you know, she's an enthusiast. She's been a bit bowled over by Jonny. She was always mad about the arts. It doesn't mean anything. Last night I thought perhaps you were a little distressed — and, of course, she is provocative."

Emma said quickly, "Last night I — I didn't feel well. It was nothing to do with Paola." She felt her face flushing. So now Jonny's and Paola's attraction for each other was plain for all to see. Her sense of mortification was complete.

"I guess marriage isn't all beer and skittles," said Kit.

"Oh, it's all right," said Emma. "When are you going to get married, Kit?"

Kit laughed. "Not for years. I'm too happy playing the field," he said.

Emma laughed a little wryly. She felt she understood Kit. He was lucky. He was fancy free and he hadn't a care in the world.

"Tell me more about the *palio*," Emma said.

Kit had agreed with Paola to enter

Siena by one of the ancient gateways known as the Porta Camollia, set in the medieval wall which encircled the city, and to park the car on the outskirts of an ornamental garden. It was here after making a few circuits of the garden that they finally saw Paola's red car and the four of them joined up again.

They had arrived at the very hottest part of the day. As she got out of the hot car, Emma felt as though she was getting into a hotter oven.

She was wearing a pink dress, flower patterned, plainly cut. It fortunately did not show creases but she felt it was sticking to her. She shook out her skirt and wiped her hot face with a tissue. She hoped she looked as cool as Paola, who did not appear to feel the heat at all.

They crossed the gardens which were crowded with strollers, clearly visitors like themselves, and soon they were in the narrow streets of the old part of the town and back in the Middle Ages. The streets were barely wide enough for a small car to pass and there was, in fact, little traffic. Only pedestrians like themselves thronged up and down the steep alleyways. Here and there the narrow black buildings opened up into a small square where palaces and churches and imposing private houses or offices were hung with gaudy red and gold banners.

Paola threaded her way through the maze of streets, the others straggling along behind her. Emma was conscious of Jonny walking along by her side, not looking at her or speaking to her. Their silence was like a sword between them.

She ignored him equally, looking about her with a false liveliness, addressing her remarks to Kit. She stared down curving alleys with a promise of adventure around the corner, into dark halls and courtyards, through open archways. She wondered aloud what it would be like to live in the top stories of the narrow buildings where the washing was sometimes suspended, to be able to put out your hand and practically touch your neighbour's from the other side of the street.

Paola led them down a short narrow lane. They went down some steps, under a canvas covering and came through the tunnel into the Piazza del Campo which was literally the centre of the city, the square where all roads met.

Opposite them was the town hall in all its fourteenth-century battlemented grandeur, with scarlet-draped seats set in front of it for the town dignitaries.

The Piazzo del Campo of Siena is in the curving shape of a shell. For the day of the *palio* it becomes an arena.

All around the square, covering the shops and cafés up to the first story, tiered seats had been built. Above the seats were the balconies, draped with banners and flags of the old houses and palaces which faced on to the square. The road round the square had been barricaded off. In the middle, stallholders had already begun to set up their fruit and soft-drink stands and small boys wearing newspaper hats to keep off the sun had already perched themselves on the walls and railings. They would have a long wait but it would be a good view.

Cafés had brought out tables and umbrellas in the roadway and it was at one of these restaurants that Paola suggested they should eat.

They sat themselves well in the shade.

The sun was now beating down fiercely, although one part of the square was already in deep shadow and here ardent supporters of the race were beginning to cluster.

Kit ordered some cold white wine and they drank it gratefully. "I know what you would like," Kit said, glancing up from the menu and across at Emma. "Melon and *prosciutto*."

"You don't know what I would like at all," Emma said gently. "You can't read my mind."

"I can always try," Kit said lightly. "I am sure it is a very nice little mind behind that pretty little face."

"*I* would like melon and *prosciutto*," said Paola interrupting.

The three of them argued amicably over what they were going to eat. Only Jonny was silent. He was half-turned away from the table, looking into the square, but the expression on his face was set. Emma, noting it, thought, 'Perhaps his ride wasn't as happy as it should have been.' Even Paola seemed subdued.

The waiter came and they gave their order, and Paola began talking to Jonny and telling him about the history of the race.

Emma tried to listen but Kit was angling for her attention. "You don't want to listen to all that stuff," he said, "history is bunk, as Mr. Ford said." He tapped his foot on the ground beneath the table. "Feel this, like concrete. I shouldn't like to race on it."

At this moment they were interrupted by one of Paola's friends who had been walking by and who now greeted Paola with delighted cries of recognition. It was the same girl whom Paola had met in the skirt shop in Florence, only now she was accompanied by her husband, a tall dark young man.

When they had walked on, arm in arm, Paola said, looking after them, "They have just come back from their honeymoon. They have not been married very long." She glanced at Jonny. "How long have you been married, Jonny?"

Emma looked down at her plate of melon and ham which the waiter had just brought. She heard Jonny say carelessly, "Oh, about a month," and looked up to meet Kit's eyes. He was looking at her with a puzzled, quizzical expression.

"Then you must have got married just before you came to Italy!" Paola said. "You are on your honeymoon, too!" She laughed and Emma looked at her quickly. The laugh and the remark seemed tinged with sarcasm. Paola's eyes as they met hers were bright and curious. She thinks I do not know, that I do not understand her double talk, Emma thought miserably, and wondered how anyone who appeared so sweet and serene could really be so mean. She wished she had had the nerve to walk in on them when she had seen them in the studio, but she had been too distressed and too much of a coward. But soon she would tackle Jonny about it. She wanted them to know that she knew, that she was not after all a blind, hoodwinked ninny.

"Oh yes, our honeymoon," Jonny said. He too looked at Emma. "I guess you could call it that. We always wanted to spend our honeymoon in Italy, didn't we, Emma?"

"Did we?" Emma murmured, hating his tone and his mocking. She did not look at him but turned instead to Kit.

Later Kit said to her sotto voce under cover of Paola's talk, "So you are not such an old experienced married woman as you like to make out!" He laughed at her gently.

The waiter now was hanging around their table waiting to clear it and them away. Other tables and umbrellas and chairs which had been set in the roadway had been removed and the roadway was being sprinkled with water to lay the dust.

The indefinable excitement in the air had increased, and Emma, despite her emotional turmoil, was affected by it. There was plenty to stare at. More and more people were walking round the square in a slow rubber-necking perambulation. People staring at people. There were all kinds. All kinds of Sienese, an occasional one in medieval dress, two-coloured tights, a swinging cloak who walked purposefully by; others, fervent *contradaioli*, supporters of their district, who wore their emblem embroidered on a scarf round the neck; all kinds of other Italians, the pale ones from the city, the sunburnt from the beaches, and all kinds of tourists like themselves, ghastly English ones who spoke in high-pitched voices and wore funny sun hats, and ghastly gum-chewing Americans, slung about with cameras like a cartoonist's dream. There were as well the unobtrusive ones to which kind Emma hoped they belonged. But as she looked at her companions, she did not think they looked eccentrically of their country. Paola was Italian, of course, but she could have been French, she looked in fact cosmopolitan. Both Kit and Jonny, in their light-coloured slacks and pale shirts looked elegant.

For a moment, Emma allowed her eyes to rest on Jonny. He was standing staring into the centre of the square with a look of absorption on his face. As she looked at his strong profile, every line of which she felt she knew by heart, the way his black hair grew at the back of his neck, curling into shape even when it was long, as it was now, when he needed to visit the barber, the sinewy strength of his shoulders beneath the thin silk shirt, the way he stood and moved all added up to a physical perfection which had an unbearable power to move her. She was full of yearning and sadness. She knew that her hatred of the night before had been a passing storm. She would always love him, whatever he was. However much she would want to salvage her wounded pride, she was stuck with him for keeps.

Jonny moved and she looked away from him quickly in case her eyes gave her away.

A girl with long blonde hair walked by, surrounded by a cohort of young men. She was attired in a form-fitting gold brocade dress which flashed and glittered in the sunlight. She looked very proud and annoyed at all the wolf whistles she was receiving.

"Cabaret artist from Rome," said Kit out of the side of his mouth to Emma. "She has a car to match that dress." Later still, on their own stroll round the town, they were to see the car, lined with white leather and white fur, its bodywork lacquered with a rough diamond-like finish, glittering like a million sequins, or the frosting on a Christmas tree decoration.

For a brief, fleeting moment, Emma envied the fantasy of such a girl's life. She wished she could soar up into the blue sky, out of her skin and her unhappiness, not think or know about Jonny any more.

They bought their seat tickets and then for an hour or so they wandered about the streets of Siena.

They went into the cathedral with its strange black and white striped pillars and its floor of many coloured marbles worked into illustrations of different biblical and historical scenes and stories.

Kit was bored and Emma found he assumed she was bored too. But Emma was not. She liked sightseeing and she liked antiquity. She was a Londoner and took comfort from old stones steeped in history and this strange, romantic, antique city of Siena appealed to her. She could have wandered up and down, explored for days, but Kit caught hold of her arm. "Let's leave Jonny and Paola," he said, "to stare out their eyes at the pictures. Let's go back to the square and find our seats."

Jonny turned at his words and looked

at Emma. Paola heard him too. "It's time we all went back," she said.

Back in the piazza, the scene had become more crowded, the excitement more intense. The centre of the square was fast becoming a sea of black heads and the central fountain, the Fonte Gaia, was almost hidden.

The sun was lower now and the square was all in shadow. Above the old buildings the sky was the most cloudless and divine blue.

Emma, wedged between Kit and Jonny, was very hot. Now, every seat, on all the tiers all round the square, was taken. There was a great hum of noise which rose to a shout as through one of the narrow streets leading into the square a procession was seen. It was composed of the town officials of the different districts, dressed in wonderful robes, preceded and followed by bands, with pages and attendants.

The crowd cheered, the bands made a prodigious noise. On Emma's right, Kit commented freely on the costumes and the horses. On her other side, Jonny was silent and she found his silence oppressive. She turned to look at him once and their eyes locked together. His face was grim.

"We can't go on like this," he muttered. Emma could only just catch the words under the cover of the noise.

"I know we can't," she said. She turned her face to look at the procession and he addressed his next remark to her profile.

"What do you want to do?" he asked.

Emma turned to look at him again. "Isn't it rather what *you* want to do?" she said angrily. "I'll go back to England if that's what you mean!"

The town officials had marched all round the square and taken their places on the far side outside the town hall, where they made a big splash of colour. Emma fixed her eyes on them, only half-seeing them.

"I had such hopes of this year in Italy," Jonny said. "I thought it was a gift from the gods. We were friends, after all. Now we seem enemies."

The first of the *contrada* processions appeared in the square. Watching it,

Emma said, "You have turned yourself into my enemy."

Each district was represented by a drummer, two flag-bearers, a captain, two pages, a standard-bearer, followed by two pages holding flags embroidered with the emblem of the district, a giraffe, a hedgehog, a goose and so on. Then came the race-horse with a groom and the jockey who was to ride, mounted for the parade on another horse. All were attired in the richest of gold and velvet and satin robes, in all the brightest combinations of colours. With their fluted and winged sleeves, their strange puffed and plumed hats, their quilted tunics, slashed doublets, the gold and black wigs beneath the hats — they were like some medieval missal come to life.

Emma felt Jonny's hand on her arm. "Look at me, Emma, what have I done to turn myself into your enemy?"

Emma tried to shake her hand free but his fingers closed over her wrist like a vice. "You know perfectly well what you have done," she muttered, "and I'm not going to argue about it here. We can't quarrel in front of all these people."

196

"I don't give a darn about all these people," Jonny said.

The drums were throbbing monotonously, the flag-bearers were doing wonderful things with their banners, tossing them up in the air and catching them with a flourish, exchanging them, whirling them over and under their legs. The cleverest received bursts of applause from the crowd.

"No one is interested in us," said Jonny. "You're such a baby, Emma, you always get so angry. You won't discuss this thing rationally. Do you want to end it?"

Emma said, "Let go my arm. I want to look in my guide-book."

As each *contrada* passed their seats she had looked for its emblem. The hedgehog was passing by but in her agitation she couldn't find it. Suddenly a man put his hand over her shoulder. He seized the guide from her, found the hedgehog and handed the book back to her with apologies. Obviously the hedgehog's supporter behind her had been watching her futile search and could not bear it.

"No one of course is looking at us," she said to Jonny sarcastically.

Kit leant over them suddenly. "That would be worth more dead in the butcher's shop," he said, pointing to one blinkered and panoplied horse which was moving crab-wise down the track scared of the crowds and the noise.

"I don't care what sort of a free show we provide," Jonny said a moment later. "I want to thrash this thing out."

"What a place to choose!" Emma said, turning to look at him again. He turned to her and they stared at each other for a long moment, their faces masks, their eyes wary. Now indeed they were on an island, Emma thought, alone in the midst of this sea of people and noise.

"I know about you and Paola," Emma said, as there was sudden crashing of cymbals and drums. Jonny raised his eyebrows at her and waited for the noise to subside.

"I wondered if that was bothering you," he said. "People get these crushes, you know, Emma, it's only a passing phase, meaningless — " The rest of his sentence was drowned as yet another band struck up in front of them.

Emma turned and looked into the piazza. She noticed the winks some of the pages were giving the onlookers. They were cheeky looking boys and their eyes slid round mischievously. A passing phase, that was what Jonny called it, and she was supposed to accept it and think nothing of it. They had different values, she might as well understand that.

The procession was over and it was time for the race to begin. The race, twice round the square, began and ended not too far away from them.

The jockeys were still in their medieval robes as they mounted. In a great bunch, with one in the lead all the way, they went round the square at a thunderous clip. Behind Emma, the hedgehog supporter went wild and beat on her shoulders shouting, *"Riccio, riccio!"*

The horses flashed by a second time, still all in a bunch, still with the hedgehog in the lead. Jonny's attention now was fully taken up with the race. Just before the end, the hedgehog's rider fell off with exhaustion but this apparently did not disqualify him. The hedgehog had won.

Although the procession seemed to have taken hours, the race itself was over in a few minutes. Emma sat in her seat, surprised. She looked first at Jonny, then at Kit.

"That was it, kid," said Jonny.

All round them, people were standing up and many were cheering. The hedgehog supporter had leapt over the seats in front of them and into the roadway and given a big jump and hugged several of his friends and then had run off in the direction of the winning-post. A few minutes later, the winning jockey was being borne shoulder high all round the race-track, followed by cheering boys.

Paola and Jonny, Kit and Emma stood up and left the box. The crowds were pouring out into the square in a great flood. They made their way out of the square into one of the streets running out of it. But here the crowd was denser than ever. And rough. Pushing and shoving was going on all around them and Emma felt as though she was in a great sea of lava. Nobody had any manners and Paola and Jonny were forging their way ahead and she was being separated from them by the crowd. Jonny gazed over his shoulder and she shouted at him despairingly. She suddenly felt an arm round her waist. It was Kit.

"Come this way," he said, and pulled her against the wall and then down into a narrow street which clearly did not lead into the main part of the town where all the rest of the crowd were going.

Emma leaned against the wall. She was breathless and winded. The crowd had been frightening.

"We'll wait awhile," said Kit, "until the mob has dispersed. We got caught right in the rush." He looked up the narrow street into which he had drawn her.

"Shall we see where this leads?" he asked.

Emma nodded and he took hold of her hand, and they walked slowly up the cobbled street. It was long and winding. They turned a corner only to find another, but then suddenly they came into another narrow street and were caught up in a crowd again, but this was a crowd dressed up and waving banners. Strong and powerful, it swept them along with it but Emma was not scared this time, for the crowd was gay and was shouting some jingle. Obviously, these were hedgehog supporters celebrating their victory. She suddenly caught sight of the man who had sat behind her. He grinned at her and shouted something in Italian. Probably he was saying, "You are on the right team," but Emma could not distinguish the words. She smiled back and shrugged her shoulders. Kit still clung to her hand and she was grateful, otherwise she felt she would have been tossed about like jetsam.

They were swept along this street and that, still in the midst of this slightly mad throng. Emma had lost all sense of direction and so apparently had Kit.

"I don't know where the devil we are," he cried to her. The crowd had thinned a bit and he had worked his way to the outermost edge of it. When he saw an open café doorway, he drew Emma in after him.

Kit mopped his brow. "Whew!" he said. "We must have been prancing along for miles." He looked about the café.

"Why don't we sit down and have a drink?"

Emma sat down gratefully. "I wonder what happened to the others," she said.

"They are probably lost too," Kit said. He ordered some drinks for them and brought a map out of his pocket. With the waiter's help, they discovered in what street they were and how they could get back to the square where they had parked the car.

It was a fair way and it was easily another half-hour before they got there. Kit's car was there but there was no sign of Paola's.

"Ah, look," said Emma. She had seen a small piece of paper tucked into the windscreen. It was a note from Paola. She and Jonny had gone home.

"They couldn't have waited very long for us," said Kit.

"No," said Emma. The troubled feelings which had possessed her all afternoon and which had been banished for a moment by the events of the past hour suddenly redoubled in intensity.

Kit looked down at her. "Why don't we stay and have supper in Siena?" he asked. "Just you and I."

For a moment, Emma hesitated and then bravado took hold of her. "Why not?" she said. Let Jonny have something to worry about. Surely he would be disturbed when they didn't turn up for dinner at the villa?

Emma smiled at Kit. "Can we go somewhere first and have a wash? I feel a wreck."

They walked across to the Excelsior Hotel where the lobby rang with transatlantic voices and in the wash-room Emma found a packet of 'Klene 'n Dri' face tissues, discarded but half full. She availed herself of this free gift, re-made-up her face after washing off the grime of the *palio*. As she did her lips in the mirror, her eyes stared back at her, bright, wild. Deep inside her was this feeling of pain overlaid with a reckless kind of excitement.

Kit was waiting for her in the foyer. He took her arm and led her down the steps of the hotel into the square. It was dusk now and bright lights pricked the blue light. There were crowds everywhere, strolling among the gardens and fountains, past the carnival stalls selling nuts and candy and cakes. There were crowds at the café tables. They had another drink at one of these cafés. Above the dark silhouette of the buildings, the sky was pink and orange and deep blue. A cold breeze fluttered round the corner and after the intense heat of the day, Emma felt chilled suddenly and was glad of the sweater she had taken from Kit's car.

They left the café and wandered back into the old part of the town. Here the narrow streets were also crowded; bands of boys whirled by, shouting and carrying banners some of them still dressed in medieval robes which looked perfect against the background of the ancient houses.

There was no direction in their wandering. They went, hand in hand, where the fancy took them, looking in at the cake and sweet shops which also seemed, strangely enough, to be provided with bars, where the customers stood up and drank beer or orange juice; peering through mysterious doorways into shadowy Byzantine courtyards; assessing the attraction of various restaurants, all of which had their tables set outside in the streets. Sometimes they turned a corner and came upon one of these restaurants suddenly, the only sign of life in an otherwise dark and shadowy canyon. The waiters would be darting between the aisle of the two rows of tables, the customers would be chattering noisily, and would look up with interest as they passed by.

In the end, they decided on a restaurant and sat down at a table in another cobbled street under the eaves of a thirteenth-century palace, its veranda under the characteristically curved Sienese arches, ablaze with potted plants, zinnias and geraniums and carnations.

Emma was not hungry but she tried to eat the spaghetti and chicken, the salad of sweet red and green peppers which Kit had ordered.

"You're very silent, Emma," Kit remarked, pouring her another glass of Chianti.

Emma forced a smile. "I'm sorry to be so dull."

"I never said you were dull. Is your conscience bothering you? I shouldn't let it. I dare say Jonny and Paola stopped on the road somewhere to have supper."

Emma took a gulp of her wine. "Probably," she said with forced gaiety, "and anyway I have no conscience!"

Half-way on the long drive home, Kit stopped the car on the side of the road, drawing up on the grass verge under the shade of a tree. He switched off the engine and in the sudden quiet the humming of the cicadas in the hedges and fields seemed to intensify the stillness of the night.

She felt him turn towards her in the darkness of the car. "Well, Emma?" he said, a query in his voice. A feeling of inevitability stole over Emma. She had thought that perhaps this jaunt might lead to this.

Kit put out his arms and pulled her towards him and kissed her warmly on the mouth.

Emma struggled, trying to push him away. She averted her face. "Please, Kit," she said, "no."

"Why not?" Kit sounded surprised

and Emma laughed involuntarily at his question.

"I'm married, for one thing," she spoke a little tartly.

Kit made a noise something between a snort and a sniff. "You're not very happy," he said. "I believe you only got married so that Jonny could accept the Grasselli prize."

Emma was silent and Kit went on. "It explains so much about you both."

"What does it explain?"

"Well, your casualness with each other, for one thing. I think this is a *mariage de convenance*, Emma."

"Do we then appear so casual?" asked Emma slowly.

Kit countered her question with one of his own. "Why did you tell me you'd been married a year when you've really only been married a month?"

"Just silliness, I guess."

"No, because you know you don't act like newly-weds."

"I suppose we don't drool all over the place," said Emma.

"It's not a question of drooling. You're not happy with Jonny. He's probably very brilliant and all that, but he's moody and mercurial and I should think very difficult to live with. I can't understand why you are so loyal to him, Emma."

There was a small silence and then Emma said simply, "Because I happen to be in love with him, Kit."

As the words left her lips, she felt an enormous sense of relief and realised with surprise that Kit was the first person she had ever told about her love for Jonny. It was the first time she had ever said the words aloud and had not been talking to herself. "I am in love with him," she repeated.

Kit said nothing for a moment or two and then he leant forward and started the engine.

"All I can say," he said, "is that you have a very funny way of showing it. And if you were in love with me, I would hope that you would be more demonstrative." He steered the car back on to the highway and drove fast, without talking any more until they were in the Grasselli driveway.

He parked the car behind Paola's red one. He did not get out at once but caught hold of Emma's hand.

"I enjoyed the evening," he said, "even though it didn't turn out as I planned."

"I enjoyed it too," Emma said and spoke with sincerity. She had enjoyed the evening in a funny kind of way. It had been a respite. Kit had given her something else to think about. He was irresponsible and probably promiscuous but basically there was also something lovable about him. One day when he met the right girl he would settle down.

"You're nice," she said suddenly.

"So are you. You can always come and cry on my shoulder, Emma, though I don't guarantee I won't try and take advantage of you. Good night!"

Emma leaned forward and gave him a quick sisterly kiss. "Good night," she said.

She got out of the car and ran down the path which led to the studio. The wood was dark and she stumbled once or twice.

The studio was ablaze with light. She could see it sparkling through the trees. As she walked in, Jonny jumped off the couch where he had been lying and threw the book he had been reading on to the floor. He was still fully dressed and had obviously been waiting up for her.

He took a step towards her and he looked so angry that she fell backwards, feeling he might almost strike her.

"Where have you been?" he demanded. He looked at his watch. "Look at the time!"

Emma took refuge in flippancy. "I've been to Siena," she said. "You should go sometime. It's a nice town." She took off her sweater. "We got lost in the crowd," she added.

"Lost in the crowd!" Jonny cried angrily. "We're going to have this out, Emma. You deliberately stayed behind with Kit Sundine. It was perfectly obvious you had a rendezvous."

# 8

EMMA looked at Jonny in amazement. "What do you mean?" she cried. "A rendezvous? Kit rescued me from the crowd. We got left behind. You did not even look round to see what had happened to me."

"Indeed I did," Jonny said. "I looked behind me to see where you were and was just in time to see you disappearing up a back street with Kit Sundine's arm round your waist. A very convenient way of getting lost."

"We got lost afterwards," Emma said. "Kit suggested we take that side street to avoid the mob."

"Emma, I am not a complete fool. It was quite obvious to both me and to Paola that you 'got lost,' as you call it, on purpose. You did nothing but flirt with Kit and encourage his attentions all day."

"Oh!" Emma cried in rage. "You dare say all this to me when you and Paola

212

— when you have admitted that you and Paola — " she paused for breath.

"What about me and Paola?" Jonny demanded.

"You admitted at the *palio* that you were infatuated — a passing phase, I think your elegant and sophisticated expression was," Emma cried.

"I admitted I was infatuated? You're out of your mind," Jonny said slowly.

"Paola has got a schoolgirl crush on me. She admires my work, she admires me. We have quite a usual pupil-teacher relationship. That's what I told you at the *palio*. I suppose you didn't hear me properly."

"And I suppose it's quite usual in such an ideal pupil-teacher relationship for the teacher to kiss the pupil?" Emma cried. "And don't bother to deny it, Jonny Brereton! I saw you with my own eyes!"

"Then there is something the matter with your eyes," Jonny said. "Let's leave Paola out of this, shall we? Let's just stick to the issue, you, me and Kit Sundine!" His face was dark with anger and emotion.

"Oh, you arrogant man," Emma cried furiously. "You can do what you like but I have to put up with humiliation —"

"Humiliation? What sort of a fool did you make of me this afternoon?"

"That's all you care about," Emma said, "if you had waited for us —"

"We waited half an hour. But Paola knew it was useless. She knows her cousin. She knew that you had some sort of assignation, some sort of arrangement."

"She knew nothing of the sort!" Emma cried.

"And where did he make love to you? In the dark streets of Siena or in the car parked at the side of the road?"

Emma stamped her foot at him, wordless with rage. "Don't tell me he didn't make love to you! I suggest you go and look at yourself in the mirror. You've no lipstick left and your eyes have the wild and excited look of a woman who's been kissed until she's breathless."

"I'm not breathless," Emma said evenly, finding her voice at last.

"Aren't you?" asked Jonny, his voice cold and cruel. "Poor cold-hearted Emma!

And you who are so romantic about love! Can't even Kit stir you to some show of passion?"

Emma, almost beside herself with rage, lunged towards him. She wanted to pummel him, punch him. He caught her by the wrists and held her off. He looked at her as she struggled to free herself, a small smile of triumph playing about his mouth as he saw how he had roused her temper.

"At least you have some feelings," he observed, not relaxing his grip on her wrists. "You've done nothing but surprise me this trip, Emma. I, who thought I knew you so well. Retiring Emma, submissive Emma, sensible Emma, standing in the shadow of the dazzling Elizabeth . . . where have all those Emmas gone? First I find your head is stuffed with romantic nonsense, now you fall for the blandishments of a professional charmer like Kit Sundine!"

"I have not fallen for Kit Sundine," Emma panted.

"When are you going to grow up?" Jonny asked, shaking her a little. "Away from home, you let the first compliments from the first man you meet go absolutely to your head."

"I hate you, I hate you, Jonny Brereton," Emma breathed. "He hasn't gone to my head — but at least he's kind — not vile and cruel, like you are — I'm not going to stay here with you — I shall go back to England!" Her words were breathless and disjointed but Jonny understood them well enough.

"I'm not going to let you go back to England," he said.

"How can you stop me?" Emma cried wildly.

"Have you got the money for your fare?" asked Jonny gently.

"I shall cable Elizabeth when she comes back from her honeymoon."

"You won't be leaving for some weeks then?"

"I'll borrow — " Emma cried furiously. "I'll borrow from Ugo Grasselli — Kit — anyone."

"You're not going to borrow money from anyone — and you're not leaving," said Jonny with finality. He let go of her and pushed her so that she fell backwards on to the couch which was directly behind her.

Emma stared up at him resentfully, massaging her wrists. "You really are impossible, Jonny," she said.

"I impossible? It is you who have behaved abominably ever since we came here! Flinging yourself at Kit Sundine's head, trying to live up to some fanciful idea he has of you, just because when he saw you first you came dripping out of a stream — like a naiad, as he so poetically put it. I'm not completely oblivious, Emma. Don't think I haven't known whom you wanted to dazzle with your new clothes, for whom you are trying to change your own personality. But this play-acting doesn't suit you nor do the bright colours — you're a pastel type girl — "

"I'm not!" Emma cried. "I'm not play-acting either and I've never wanted to dazzle Kit Sundine. This is the real me, Jonny. I don't believe you've ever properly known me. To you, I've always been an extension of Elizabeth." She stood up.

"You're right," Jonny said slowly. "I

don't believe I have ever really known you."

Emma turned away from him and walked slowly across the room to the staircase. "I'm not going to argue with you any more," she said. "It's completely pointless. You don't believe me — and I don't believe you."

Upstairs in her room, Emma wandered about, too distressed to go to sleep. She pulled out her new clothes and laid them out on the bed. They were beautiful. She undressed and feverishly began trying them on. She looked at herself in the mirror with critical eyes. Jonny's remarks had mortified her. But he was wrong. Bright colours did suit her. She was not a pastel girl. She was not play acting. For the first time in her life she had bought clothes away from Elizabeth's influence. Elizabeth always wore extreme fashions, model clothes. Emma had always known they were not for her but her own taste had been governed by Elizabeth's love of plainness and formality.

'And I'm not like that either,' thought Emma, gazing at herself in her red dress. 'I would rather look pretty than smart.'

She took off the red dress and put the others away, her mind remembering and ranging over all Jonny's remarks. He had had the barefaced effrontery to deny there was anything between himself and Paola. And to accuse her of throwing herself at Kit Sundine. It would be funny if she were not so bitterly unhappy.

It was almost as though Jonny were jealous of Kit and yet she could not flatter herself it was because of any feelings he had for her. But she was his wife and his pride resented her supposed interest in Kit or his in her.

Emma got into bed and lay awake in the dark, staring up at the raftered ceiling. No light shone up from down below in the studio so Jonny too must have gone to bed.

The more Emma thought over their scene together, the more she marvelled at the fact of his jealousy and the more the hurtful and wounding things she had said moved to the back of her mind. Jonny was jealous of Kit! Of her interest in Kit. She felt he had placed a weapon in her hand. And why had he bothered to deny his relationship with Paola? Perhaps because he was ashamed of it — because it was a passing phase — a sudden temptation? Emma fell asleep at last, resolutely pushing wild, hopeful surmises out of her head.

It was as well she did for Jonny's attitude in the next few days made her understand that she had imagined and surmised too much.

The morning after their midnight quarrel he did not come upstairs with her usual coffee. He worked before breakfast and did not join her on the terrace until she was almost through her coffee and *brioches*. He gave her a cold, polite 'good morning' and a steady glance from his dark eyes. Later he spoke about the *palio* but there was no reference to their scene of the night before. It might almost never have happened.

He spoke impersonally about Siena, said he'd like to go back there and make some sketches and ruminated vaguely as to how it could be arranged. Emma felt she was talking to a stranger. Jonny had withdrawn himself to some fastness of the spirit. If he had regretted showing his hand last night, there was no sign

220

of that either. But the barriers were up, this time for good. He mentioned Kit in passing in his conversation, blandly, with no oblique or sidelong reference and when Kit came over with Paola, he greeted him pleasantly as though he were genuinely pleased to see him.

Kit said, "I'm driving into Florence this morning. I thought you'd like a lift, Emma."

"Yes, please," Emma said, watching Paola as she arranged herself in her chair. She was giving Jonny a two-hour sitting again this morning.

Jonny leant forward and took hold of Paola's chin and tilted it a little bit to the side. He then picked up her hand and arranged it carefully on the arm of the chair. Admittedly, he made these gestures as though Paola were a wax figure and Emma had seen him make them many times before, but somehow there was an intimacy about them which tore at her heart-strings.

She turned away and looked at Kit. His eyes had a curiously soft, pitying expression in them, she thought. "When are you leaving?" she asked mechanically.

"Whenever you are ready," Kit said promptly.

So their days went on as before though the ache in Emma's heart grew more unbearable. She went into Florence most days for her Italian lessons. She heard from the Campanellis that they would be coming back soon and would want to start their English conversation again. She read a lot and she worked hard.

Jonny too was working hard. Paola's portrait was beautiful. He was pleased with it and so was Paola. 'It is painted with love,' thought Emma, looking at it one day, noting the tender quality of the skin tones, the delicate tendrils of hair, the curve of the face delineated with such warm precision.

"Not bad at all," said Kit, standing beside her. "Your husband can paint, Emma."

"Yes," Emma sighed, faintly, imperceptibly. She moved away from the easel. It was late afternoon and the studio was full of golden splintered light. She and Kit had just come in from sunbathing in the garden. Paola and Jonny had gone to see Loudon Brighouse in Florence, the American painter whom Emma had still not met. Sometimes she wondered if he really existed or was just an excuse made up for Jonny and Paola to be alone together.

Emma began pulling up the shutters, flooding the place with light and sun. Kit went back to the villa and she moved about the studio, tidying up. The gardener had brought her some flowers and she arranged them in a big copper urn, getting some comfort from the colour and beauty of them. She put the urn against the white wall and stepped back to see the effect. She looked around the studio. It could be such a fun place to live in, she thought sadly. It was a doll's house of a home. For two people in love, it could be paradise. But two strangers live here, Emma said to herself. "Two strangers," she said the words aloud, her heart sad, "and they live in different parts of the house."

She wandered out on to the terrace and into the gardens. She often walked in the garden at this time of the day. It was cooler and the flowers seemed to release their scent on the early evening air. She rambled on, along the gravelled walks bordered with trim edges of yew to the far lawn where a row of cypress stood sentinel. From the lawn, steps led up to a kind of terrace covered with a pergola up which a grape vine grew and also another creeper covered in beautiful pale mauve flowers. Emma had learnt some days previously from one of the gardeners that this exotic looking thing was merely a humble potato. She walked under the pergola until she came to the final archway. From this little eminence you got a fine vista of the house. It was a good way away so that you could see its fine proportions outlined against its bower of trees. The driveway curved away from it into the distance under the trees.

Emma saw the gleam of Paola's red sports car parked in the driveway. So they must be back. As she was thinking this she saw them walking up the steps of the house. They had their arms around each other's waists, Jonny's blue shirt contrasting prettily with Paola's pink dress.

Emma turned back under the archway, sick at heart. So it was still going on, as she had known it was, in her heart of hearts. And yet the evidence of it still made her feel physically ill. She walked slowly back to the studio wondering how she was going to cope with her feelings. Should she tell Jonny that she really couldn't stand it any longer and must go back to England?

When she got back to the studio, she found to her surprise that Jonny was already there. He was standing in front of his portrait of Paola. With his finger he rubbed out something in the background.

"I'm not absolutely pleased with the eyes," he said, as Emma came in. "They're not quite right." Emma noticed that he had changed his shirt. He was now wearing a white one. Got lipstick on it, she supposed bitterly.

"They look perfectly fine to me," she said.

"I'm going to get Brighouse over to come and look at it," Jonny went on. "I thought perhaps we might ask him over to dinner one night. I don't suppose

225

Paola would mind."

"So I'm actually going to meet the great Brighouse," said Emma sarcastically.

Jonny turned to stare at her. "I didn't know you were so keen to meet him," he said. "You probably won't like him, anyway. Paola didn't."

"Then how does she manage to work with him?" Emma asked.

"She doesn't," Jonny spoke absently.

"But she's always going into Florence with you when you visit Brighouse," Emma said in surprise.

"Well, she doesn't come to Brighouse's studio," said Jonny without interest. "She never has — after that first time."

"Well, where does she go?" Emma asked, astonished.

Jonny turned to look at her again. "I haven't the faintest idea," he said. "I'm not responsible for Paola's movements, Emma, though you appear to think I am. I suppose she has friends in Florence whom she visits, or she shops, or something. She was kind enough to offer to take me in whenever I wanted to go and as I am not as energetic about the bus as you are, I've kept her to her promise."

"I see," said Emma.

"When shall we ask Brighouse?" said Jonny.

Emma shrugged. "I don't mind when," she said. "Perhaps you had better consult Paola."

"I'll leave it to you to arrange with her," Jonny said. "We had better have supper here in the studio and Paola and Kit can come if they want to, otherwise it can just be the three of us."

"All right," Emma agreed, "I'll ask her to-night."

But they did not see Paola again that day. Kit came over later.

"Can I have supper with you?" he asked. "Paola has gone careering off to Florence. I wanted to go with her but she wouldn't let me." Kit looked a trifle put out, Emma thought. He added, "Sometimes she's as stubborn as a mule. I think I'm going to phone Uncle Ugo later on this evening. What shall I say if he asks about the portrait?"

"Tell him it's coming along fine. Nearly finished," said Jonny cheerfully.

Paola did not appear early in the studio the next morning and Emma left for Florence without seeing her. When she returned at lunch-time, she found a disgruntled Jonny.

"Paola never turned up for her sitting this morning," he said irritably, "and here I am bursting to get on with her portrait. It's so nearly finished."

"Why didn't she come over?" asked Emma, dropping her books and handbag on to the table and kicking off her high-heeled sandals.

"I don't know." Jonny lit himself a cigarette. "I can't even make out from Mario whether she's in the house or not. Her car's there but Mario, one minute, says *she's* not and the next minute looks evasive and silly and says, 'When the signorina come down . . . '"

"Where's Kit?" asked Emma.

"He's hopped it somewhere too. At least his car is not around."

"Maybe they've gone somewhere together," suggested Emma.

"Well, it's a nerve and a bore," said Jonny angrily. "Paola knows perfectly well I want to get the thing finished. I want to get on with some other work now." He looked at her for a moment without

228

speaking, his eyes moving from her feet, bare on the marble floor, to her face, in a manner he had now, at once intimidating and appraising. It always made Emma feel less than nothing. "When you have had something to eat," Jonny went on, "I want you to go over to the house and find out what has happened to Paola. No doubt with your fluent and excellent Italian, you will be able to get to the bottom of Mario's rigmarole."

Emma said nothing and helped herself to the bread and cheese and fruit of which her lunch was going to consist. She took her plate and walked towards the terrace. At the doorway she paused. "You don't have to sneer at my Italian," she said. "I have learnt quite a lot."

"I wouldn't presume to sneer," Jonny said in mock humility.

"Have you and Paola quarrelled?" Emma asked.

"What would we quarrel about?"

"You know perfectly well. Any number of things, including your perfect pupil-teacher relationship," Emma said, and walked out into the sunshine.

Almost before she had finished her

meal, Jonny was standing in front of her.

"Will you go now and find out if she's coming over this afternoon?" His voice was almost pleading, "can't settle to any work until I know one way or the other."

"All right," Emma rose from her chair, her tone a little ungracious.

Obviously, Jonny and Paola must have quarrelled, and now he was worried about it.

The front door of the house was always open, and when she had walked up the flight of steps and across the veranda, she went straight into the hall without knocking or ringing the bell.

A maid was polishing in the hall, and Emma asked her where the signorina was. She was in her room, the maid answered, rising politely from the floor and nodding vaguely up the stairs.

Emma went boldly up. She knew Paola's room. She knocked at the door and heard Paola call out, *"Avanti!"* obviously thinking she was one of the maids.

Emma put her head round the door, "May I come in?"

Paola was lying on her bed, fully

dressed. The windows were shuttered and the room was dim but Emma was clearly able to see that Paola had been crying. Her eyes were red and swollen.

"Is anything the matter?" Emma asked, edging her way into the room.

Paola, who had half-raised herself from her pillows when she saw Emma, now fell back again.

"No-o — " she said in a husky voice. "Nothing's the matter. I didn't — didn't feel very well this morning . . . "

Emma shut the door and leaned against it. "Jonny's very upset too," she said evenly.

"Is he?" Paola murmured indifferently.

"He wants to finish the painting," Emma went on.

Paola stirred on the bed restlessly but she said nothing.

"Do you think you will be coming over to the studio this afternoon?" Emma asked.

"No — I — I don't think I can," Paola said hesitantly.

"Jonny will be very annoyed," Emma said, "he is longing to finish the painting."

Paola sat up on the bed. "Look at my face," she said, "would Jonny want to paint me like this with my eyes all red — like this?" She touched her face with her long brown fingers. "You must tell him I'm sorry, Emma. Maybe to-morrow — "

Emma hesitated by the door. There seemed nothing else to be said.

"Don't go," Paola said hurriedly in a low voice. "I am in such a predicament, Emma."

"I know," Emma spoke slowly. "I can guess. I am not blind, Paola." She felt faint, as though the room was suffocating her.

"Is it so obvious then — that I am in love? You are clever to guess, Emma. It has been terrible these past few weeks keeping it to myself. You don't know how I have wanted to tell you. And then I thought, 'No, you would feel about it — like Kit . . . '"

"Does Kit know?" asked Emma, a sudden sharp pain of humiliation going through her.

"I had to tell him everything. He was threatening to go and see my father. He became suspicious, you see, and he feels responsible for me, silly thing. He is not my guardian. But I begged him not to — all sorts of mad ideas have gone through my mind. I have wanted to run away — "

"And where would you run to?" It was Kit who walked into the room without ceremony and overheard Paola's last words. "What are you doing fusting away in your room still, Paola?"

Paola did not answer his last question but his first.

"You know now perfectly well where I would run to.

It would be San Carlo," she said. "Is everything all right, Kit?" she added.

"More or less," Kit said.

"I'll leave you now," Emma said. She felt suddenly that the two cousins wanted to be alone, that Kit had some communication to impart which was for Paolo's ears alone.

"Let us go out for supper," Paola said eagerly. "You and Jonny, Kit and I."

She seemed suddenly gayer. Confession is good for the soul, Emma thought.

"Where shall we go?" Kit asked.

"The Caravella! Where else?" Paola said.

"I'll ask Jonny," Emma said stiffly. Walking back to the studio she told herself feverishly that she must know what Jonny and Paola intended to do. Paola had talked of running away. She knew then that she must turn her back on Jonny. Obviously they had had a quarrel. But what about? Renunciation? Their situation?

She would say to Jonny, 'Look, this deceit has gone on long enough. I have got to know what you intend doing,' and supposing he said, 'Nothing!' What then was she, Emma, going to say and do?

But somehow when she faced Jonny in the studio, the words, the accusation, would not come.

"You look very pale," Jonny remarked. "Are you feeling all right?"

"I'm okay," Emma said abruptly.

"Is it the heat?" Jonny went on.

"I'm okay," Emma repeated. She felt his tone of concern was completely hypocritical. "I like the heat. In any case, please don't bother about me," she added. "Paola is not coming to sit

234

for you this afternoon. She's not well or upset or something."

Jonny's face darkened while she spoke and he threw down his brushes in irritation.

"I'm sick of this portrait," he cried. "I want to finish it — put it away, get it out of my system. I want to start some other work — something big. I feel ideas bursting out of me."

Emma gazed at him. "You're very, very disciplined about work, aren't you?" she said. "It's the one sure thing I know about you — your relationship with your work."

Jonny gave her a sharp look before picking up his brushes again. "I'm disciplined about other things as well," he said. "I've been disciplined all my life about what I want to do and what I can do. You know the hardest thing about work? It's sticking at it — putting the bottom on the chair, putting words on paper, putting paint on canvas. I've admired you for sticking at your Italian. It would have been so easy for you to give up after you had learnt to say '*grazie*' and '*buon giorno*.' But no, you've gone into Florence and not sunbathed in the garden, and learnt your grammar and irregular verbs. You'll be reading Dante in the original before long. It's sticking at work that counts," he said again, touching up the canvas in front of him gently. "That's what is hard."

"You don't seem to find it hard," Emma observed, allowing herself to study his profile.

"That's because I have a routine," Jonny said, "but don't think I don't want to break the routine and just lie around basking in the sun doing nothing. Because I do. Often. But I know that I mustn't — if I'm to achieve anything. It always makes me sick when people come up to me and say, 'Oh, how wonderful to create,' waving their arms about vaguely as though it was all done with a wand! It's blood, sweat and tears which count."

"How much longer do you have to spend on Paola's portrait?"

"Perhaps another sitting, perhaps two," Jonny replied.

"I'm just not quite there with it. I'm not absolutely satisfied, and I really want

Ugo to be pleased. If I am, I think he will be."

At the mention of Paola, he had become bad-tempered again, Emma noticed, and he still seemed angry in the evening when the four of them went to the Caravella. He chided Paola not gently but brusquely in front of the others. Paola, however, seemed indifferent to his anger.

"Oh, you are fussing too much, Jonny," she said. "Why not call the portrait finished? It looks finished to me. You are such a perfectionist." Jonny scowled but said nothing more.

The Caravella was the restaurant to which Paola had taken Emma on their first shopping expedition and Emma herself had lunched there, but at night-time it seemed subtly different. There were soft lights among the tables outside. Inside, each table had a pink lamp. There was a small dance floor and a three-piece band, very lively in its playing.

"What happened to your friend the pianist?" Emma asked idly, noticing that another young man and not Signor Valli was at the piano.

Paola looked a little wooden as she

answered, "Oh, he's got another job — a very good one — with another band. They're going to America at the end of the season — for a tour all round the States."

Kit leant over the table. "Would you like to dance?" he asked Emma. They danced for quite a while through a series of South American numbers, but finally the band gave a final flourish and went off for a rest. Kit led Emma back to their table. As they arrived, Emma heard Jonny say distinctly and furiously to Paola:

"But you can't do this to me!"

He was white with anger and Paola's face was also flushed and furious. "I have never been spoken to like that before in my life," she cried.

"No," Jonny said, "because you always have your own way. It is time someone did speak to you like that."

Paola tossed her head like a sulky child. "Well, you're not going to," she said. "You're an employee of my father's."

Jonny laughed harshly. "I am not an employee of your father's."

"He hired you to paint my portrait,"

238

said Paola. "If I say I don't want to sit any more, that's my concern. It's none of yours. I consider the picture is finished and that's that. My father will send you a cheque. You don't have to worry about your money."

"I am the one to judge when the picture is completed," Jonny said evenly.

Paola looked across at Emma. "I am sorry about all this argument," she said, "but Jonny is angry because I am going to San Carlo to-morrow."

"To-morrow?" Emma repeated in surprise.

"Yes, I only made up my mind this afternoon," Paola said. "Kit is coming with me. We will drive down to-morrow morning. It takes about two hours and we will get there at lunch-time."

"And when will you come back?" Emma asked.

Paola shrugged and looked vague. "I shall probably stay there for the rest of the season," she said.

"Can't you finish the portrait in September when Paola comes back?" asked Kit, turning to Jonny.

"No," Jonny said, unequivocally, not

explaining. But Emma knew how he hated to return to a canvas after he had finished with it. She knew too how much he longed to finish Paola's portrait now.

"Jonny is not always reasonable about these things," she said half apologetically, trying to remove some of the strain in the atmosphere, and yet she felt that Jonny and Paola were quarrelling about more than their portrait. That was only part of the iceberg which was showing.

"Reasonable!" Jonny flashed at her. "I'm being perfectly reasonable. I just want Paola to stay here for two more days to let me finish, and then she can go to Timbuctoo for all I care."

"What about your own work — your own painting?" Emma turned to Paola.

Paola shrugged. "I feel I need a rest," she said. "I have worked hard, and I have worked all my creative energy out of my system. Now I need to be recharged — like a battery — with some of the sea and sun of San Carlo."

Jonny said nothing but looked scornful. Emma remembered Elena's words about Paola's lack of application and her dilettantism. Still, if Paola did not want to go on painting, why should she? She was not a dedicated artist, she did not have a living to make, and that was all there was to it.

"I do think we could stay a little longer," Kit said.

"You know perfectly well I can't," Paola almost snapped at him. "I want to go to San Carlo to-morrow and I'm going to-morrow. I never wanted my portrait painted anyway. I'm not interested in it and I don't care whether it is ever finished or not."

"Neither do I," said Jonny evenly. "I have only wanted to please your father for the interest he has taken in my work."

The argument went on longer but the outcome was unchanged. Paola was determined to leave early in the morning and Jonny absolutely refused to touch the picture again in September when she would be returning.

"In any case I may not be here in September," he said. "I may go to Rome."

Paola laughed at this. "Perhaps I will not be here in September either," she said. "Who can tell?"

They left the Caravella immediately they had eaten. All four of them had been made uncomfortable by the argument and wanted to part as soon as they could.

When they arrived at the villa, Paola said to Emma, "I must say good-bye to you now. I will not see you in the morning." She shook hands formally.

Kit was more demonstrative. He put his hands on Emma's shoulders and kissed her. "I shall only say '*au revoir*,'" he said. "I may come back here in a few days. When will you be going to Rome? I shall be going back there in September, you know. We must not lose touch. Anyway I will let you know when I am coming back here."

"Good-bye, good-bye," Jonny said impatiently, keeping his hands resolutely in his pockets. "I expect we will all meet again very soon. I shall write to your father, Paola, and tell him that the portrait is not finished and that you refused to sit for me any longer."

"And I shall tell him — " began Paola — "I shall tell him the truth." She paused a moment and then added "I shall tell him the portrait *is* finished but that you will keep adding extra details which are quite unnecessary."

Jonny and Emma were silent as they walked back through the wood to the studio.

So now they were really going to be alone! Emma's head was filled with this enormous thought, and yet she felt no triumph, no elation. In some strange way, she felt sorry for Jonny. He had lost a battle. Paola had tired of him along with her painting. The artist as well as art had been booted out of her life. Jonny was worthy of better treatment, cruel and unkind and unfaithful to her though he had been. Paola did not deserve him.

"Spoilt creature!" Jonny said when they were back in the studio. He was staring at Paola's portrait still on his easel. Very deliberately he took it down and walked over and put it face to the wall at the other side of the studio.

Emma looked at him with pity in her eyes. She wondered how much he was suffering. She thought, 'I wish I could exorcise Paola for you, make you forget her — for your sake as well as my own!'

The next morning at breakfast, she said, "What about Loudon Brighouse? Would you like to ask him to supper to-night?"

Jonny looked up from the ripe golden peach he was peeling neatly and carefully.

"Why to-night?" he asked. "Are you so scared of being alone with me? Is it so boring?"

Emma looked at him uncomfortably. It had occurred to her that it would be their first night alone together for several weeks. A third person might make it less difficult.

"It's not that," she said hesitantly.

"Well, what is it, Emma? Why can't we have a cosy, intimate dinner together? Why must we ask Loudon Brighouse?"

"For heaven's sake," Emma cried, exasperated. "It is you who wants the man to come here, after all, to look at your portrait."

"Well, I don't want him to come to-night. I plump for the cosy intimate dinner. Let's plan ourselves a lovely menu and over it we can sort out our affairs and decide what we are going to do."

244

"All right," Emma murmured faintly. At his words her heart contracted painfully.

"But let's be honest with each other," Jonny said. "That's a promise. Are you going into Florence this morning?"

Emma nodded. "I have always been honest with you," she said.

"I doubt that." Jonny put the last of his peach in his mouth. "I'm going sketching this morning. I thought I might wander down towards the village and try and capture some country scene or another. I feel like a change of climate."

When Emma arrived back from Florence later in the morning, she was surprised to see Paola's car still in the driveway.

For one wild moment she wondered and hoped that Paola had gone in Kit's car and left her own behind, and then she knew that this would never happen. Paola adored her little red 'fire-wagon' as she called it and would want it at San Carlo.

Paola had, after all, not gone to San Carlo in time for lunch.

Her heart beating, Emma walked quickly down the path to the studio.

From the terrace, she heard Paola's laughter. As she walked into the studio, she saw they were holding each other's hands and Paola was laughing up into Jonny's face.

When Jonny saw Emma, he let Paola go. Quickly Paola looked at Emma. "I came to apologise for my rudeness last night," she said without any hesitation. "Kit told me I was abominable. And I have had a brilliant idea to which Jonny, bless him, has agreed. We are all going to San Carlo. You two are coming down for the week-end — a long week-end, in the English style. Jonny can take the portrait with him, show my father, and finish it off there. San Carlo will do us all good. And besides, thinking it over, I decided my father perhaps would like to see the portrait before it is completely finished. Also," she added and laughed a little wryly, "Kit told me he thought my father would be on Jonny's side. You will enjoy San Carlo, Emma."

"Don't you think it is a good idea?" asked Jonny.

"Yes," said Emma without enthusiasm. Paola did not seem to notice Emma's lack of excitement.

"Do your packing this afternoon," she said. "We plan to drive down about five which means we will get there in time for supper. I shall go and telephone now and tell them to be prepared for us. We have plenty of room and you will be very comfortable."

When she had gone, Jonny said, "If you are wondering how Paola and I came to be holding hands in such a friendly manner, I can explain — "

"You don't have to explain anything," said Emma sharply. "I don't want to know."

"Well then, don't look so wounded," Jonny returned.

"I don't want to go to San Carlo," said Emma. "I think you might at least have had the courtesy to ask me before agreeing."

"It's partly out of consideration for you that we're going," retorted Jonny. "You've been looking so odd lately that I think a sea breeze and some cool air would do you good."

"I don't want to go," Emma repeated stubbornly. "You can go by yourself."

"I am doing no such thing," said Jonny. "We are going together. It would have been churlish to refuse Paola. She is like a child. She came full of the most abject humility and apologies. The invitation to San Carlo was her way of asking to be forgiven. I lost my temper idiotically too, last night. Both of us, I suppose, were strung up. Perhaps we all need a rest. You will enjoy it when you get there, Emma."

# 9

PAOLA drove herself down to San Carlo, leaving the others to follow, as soon as they had packed, in Kit's car.

"I am in a hurry to get there," she said, "so I won't wait for you." Watching the way she roared off down the drive, Emma wondered whether she would arrive in San Carlo in one piece.

She moved distractedly about the studio trying to think what she would need for the beach. It was so clear to her what had happened. Jonny and Paola had quarrelled; now they were reconciled, and the reconciliation was to be made sweeter by this visit to San Carlo.

"Hurry up," Jonny said impatiently, looking at her. "You're walking about like a zombie. Come on, tell me where your things are, and I'll help you to pack."

His own clothes he had already packed and his suitcase, his painting things and the carefully wrapped canvas were stowed away in Kit's car.

He followed Emma up the stairs to her bedroom. Her suitcase was open on the bed.

Jonny went to the wardrobe and pulled out her pink dress, "Do you want this? Remember we'll only be there three or four days."

He began doing her packing for her good-humouredly, his thin supple fingers folding her clothes with neat precision.

"I haven't got a bathing-suit," said Emma.

"Oh, never mind that, Paola will lend you one I expect. Go and get your toothbrush and your flannel. Where's the case you keep all your pots and lotions in? Do cheer up, Emma. Anyone would think you were going to a funeral."

'I feel I am,' Emma thought but did not say so aloud. 'Why don't I stand up for myself?' she chided herself. 'Why don't I say, "I won't be treated like this, I won't be pushed around and humiliated any more!"?' But under Jonny's high pressure, she seemed to have no will-power, and in a very short while, she found her case was packed and put in the car, and she was sitting beside Kit, with Jonny in the back seat, and they were all sweeping along the road in the late afternoon sunshine.

"We will be in plenty of time for supper," Kit said. "Ugo never dines before nine. I'm so glad we're all going together. We'll have a terrific week-end." He glanced down sideways at Emma.

Emma leaned her head against the back of the seat. "How lovely," she said mechanically. The shadows of the trees lining the road flicked across the car at steady intervals. They passed farm carts, laden with hay and grass, lumbering home from the fields and there was plenty of traffic: cars, bicycles, scooters. It was the end of the day and a somnolent haze was settling over the orchards and the fields of maize. Emma tried hard not to think about anything, to notice only the passing scene, the pink villa with the painted window-sills, a child, with a face like a Botticelli angel, playing in the dust at the roadside. She would not think about Jonny or Paola, or what this week-end portended.

It was dusk when they reached San Carlo. For some miles they had been driving along the coast road, under groves of pines, past hotels and bathing-cabins, strung with neon lights. Then Kit turned off the main road down a road shaded with trees, turned again into another. Behind walls, and fences, under tall pines, the lights of different villas glittered. Kit turned the car slowly into a driveway. On the gate-posts a name was lettered 'Il Cappannello della Nonna.'

"It means Grandmother's Little Cottage," Kit explained, "and it did once belong to Uncle Ugo's mother, but she is dead now but the family still come here for holidays. There are always masses of relations and friends."

The house was of stone set among lawns and shaded with tall trees including many pines. As Emma got out of the car she noticed the delicious piny scent of the air.

To the left of the house was a wide covered terrace scattered with gay chairs and low tables. People were sitting there in the dusk, and as they drove up, several of them, among them Ugo Grasselli and

Elena, rose to meet them.

There was much friendly greeting and salutation. Emma and Jonny were introduced to various people standing or sitting around. Servants came and unloaded their baggage from the car.

"But where is Paola?" cried Elena in the midst of the confusion.

"Hasn't she arrived yet?" Jonny said in surprise. "She left about an hour before us."

"I think she was stopping on the way to see someone," Kit said quickly. "She'll be here any minute."

Emma, thinking of the way Paola had driven down the drive, said, "I hope she's all right — hasn't driven into anything!"

"What has happened to Paola?" It was Ugo Grasselli now who was inquiring for his daughter.

"She had to go and see someone on the way," Kit said. "She won't be long."

"Who did she have to go and see?" Ugo Grasselli sounded puzzled.

"Some friend or another," Kit said evasively. "She didn't leave much before us — perhaps we just made better time."

Emma glanced at him in surprise.

Paola had left ages before they had.

"I'm sure you want a bath and a change," Ugo said. "We must show you your rooms, Mrs. Brereton. I am so glad that you accepted Paola's invitation to come down here." He turned to Jonny, "And I am looking forward to seeing the portrait." He indicated a servant who was carrying the carefully wrapped canvas into the house, "That is it, I take it. We must have an unveiling after dinner."

Emma and Jonny followed their host into the house. It was quite unlike the Grasselli home with all its Florentine and antique splendour.

Here all was newness and modernity with black and white marbled floors, strange shaped chairs, many bright colours. It was one-storied and sprawling with most of the rooms seeming to lead off the central entrance hall.

Ugo walked across the hall, opened a door and said, "Here is our guest bedroom. I hope you will be comfortable."

He went in, switching on lights, Emma and Jonny at his heels. The servant came in a moment later with their bags. It was a big room with a white marble floor and pale blue walls. A pale blue bathroom led off it, and there was a wide window with blue painted shutters. Twin beds were pushed close together with reading lights attached to the bed heads and a table at either side. It all looked very luxurious and comfortable.

"Have you everything you want?" asked Ugo Grasselli, standing by the door.

"I think so," said Jonny.

"If you want a dress pressed, Enrico here will take it for you," said Ugo. "We do not dine until about nine so there is no hurry."

There was a sudden noise in the hall behind him, a clatter of high heels on the marble floor, a high-pitched greeting in Italian. It was Paola.

She embraced her father and slipped her arm through his and stood at the door with him, smiling at them. Her eyes were very bright and she looked strangely excited and happy.

"So you arrived before me," she said. "I did not think you would make such good time. I got delayed with a puncture," she added quickly.

When they had gone and shut the door and left them alone, Jonny said, "I wonder what Paola is up to? She left ages before us." He walked over to the window and pushed back the shutters and stood looking out.

"Yes," said Emma non-committally. She picked up her suitcase.

Jonny turned round. "Here, let me do that," he said. "Where do you want it?" He walked over and took the suitcase from her. Their fingers touched momentarily.

"If you could put it on the rack at the foot of the bed," Emma said faintly.

Jonny did as she asked and opened the case for her. She pulled out a frock and shook it out. It was creased and needed ironing. She rang the bell and began the rest of her unpacking. Jonny also began unpacking, moving from the bedroom to the bathroom, putting out his shaving gear, hanging up his clothes.

A maid answered the bell and Emma gave her the dress. She also asked the maid if the beds could be pushed apart and a table placed between them. The girl answered in a great flood of Italian from which Emma gathered that this way of arranging twin beds was *alla matrimoniale*. "You don't like the beds *alla matrimoniale*?" the girl asked in obvious surprise.

Emma smiled and shook her head, "Please separate them," she said, "later on, when we have gone."

All this exchange had taken place in Italian which Jonny clearly had not understood. Emma did not enlighten him. 'He can find out afterwards when it's done,' she thought. She felt she could not bear to sleep so close to him, with only a few inches separating them, hearing him breathe and move. Physically, he had an overpowering effect on her. Despite everything, she was still under his spell, and she resented what she thought of as her weakness.

She felt shy, more shy than she had ever felt with him. She felt that their close proximity must be irksome to him, that he must wish more than ever that he was not tied to her by marriage.

She knew now he was in love with Paola. Else why were they here at San Carlo? Why had he submitted so meekly to Paola's change of mood, accepted her apologies so readily?

Jonny came out of the bathroom.

"Do you mind if I have a shower first?" he asked.

"No, please go ahead," Emma said politely. Jonny gave her an odd look and disappeared into the bathroom again.

The maid came back with her dress and Emma took off most of her clothes and slipped into her dressing-gown. The enforced intimacy of the next three days was going to be painful and embarrassing. Their situation had been so much easier and better in the studio where they each had their own unobtrusively separate accommodation.

She sat down in front of the dressing-table and cleaned her face with cream and lotion. She did not look up when Jonny came out of the bathroom. She heard him moving around behind her while she pinned up her hair and she caught an occasional glimpse of him in the glass. Then she stood up and turned round. She was ready to have her own bath.

Jonny, now dressed but still without

shoes or socks, was lying on the bed, smoking a cigarette, looking up at the ceiling. When she moved, however, he turned his eyes towards her. "Emma!"

She stood by the bathroom door, half turned away from him. "Emma, look at me." She forced herself to meet his glance, burning and penetrating.

"Yes, Jonny?" she said.

"When are we going to have that talk about our affairs?" he said.

"Not now," Emma said in sudden panic. She must have warning, to arm herself, gird herself. "After the week-end you can tell me."

"But I am relying on the week-end to bring things to a head," Jonny said. "We can't really go on like this, Emma. Surely you can see that?"

"I see it perfectly well," said Emma proudly.

Jonny got up from the bed and came over and put his hands on her shoulders. She flinched involuntarily as he touched her. He gave a wry smile and dropped his hands. "Of course, I am not allowed to touch you," he said bitterly. "We must be sensible about this, Emma. How am

I to get through to you when you have built such a barrier around yourself?"

"I must bathe and change," said Emma stiffly. "It is getting late."

"Okay, okay," said Jonny wearily. "I'll leave you to it. I'll go and join the others, tell them you will be ready soon."

He looked at her for a long moment, seemed about to say something else and then shrugged and left the room.

"Be sensible, indeed," muttered Emma to herself as she washed and changed and made up her face. "How can I be sensible? I am not so wordly wise, so grown-up as he is."

So this week-end was to be the culmination, San Carlo was the place he had chosen to tell her what he had wanted to do. She wondered why he had dragged it on so long and then knew that it was because he had not made up his mind before. But now he had and he had a plan or a solution. Whatever it was, it could only spell unhappiness for her. Perhaps he wanted a complete separation; perhaps he would suggest that they should stay legally married but be free to 'go their own way' in that sordid phrase, free to do as they chose with no questions asked. Emma gave a final savage tug to her dress and cinched in the belt. She was slimmer than usual. She had lost weight in the last few days.

She stepped out of the bedroom into the hall and heard an enormous buzz of sound coming from the terrace. It sounded like a party.

Ugo Grasselli rose from his long cane chair as she appeared on the edge of his gathering. He took her round and introduced her to everybody. They were an assorted bunch of relatives and friends, with variegated offspring. The Grassellis had been coming to San Carlo for years. They knew most of the residents in the villas all around them. As well there were always many of their friends from Florence and Rome staying in the hotels. There was a constant stream of visitors to 'Il Cappannello della Nonna.'

This evening when they finally sat down in the dining-room, there were twenty people sitting round the long table which was covered with a vivid pink cloth and set with gay pottery plates, bamboo-handled knives and forks, large straw-covered bottles of Chianti and wooden bowls of beautiful ripe peaches, grapes, pears and nectarines.

Jonny was sitting far away from her at the other end of the table with Paola. Kit was nearer and she was able to talk a little with him, but the men on either side of her were Italian and their English was of the scantiest. In the end, Emma decided to practise her Italian and found she was getting on very well indeed. Her lessons were paying off.

She became a little centre of attraction at her end of the table, the people around her evidently finding her accent both attractive and charming. She almost began to enjoy herself.

The dinner was very long and the guests very noisy. They shouted at each other across the table and down the table. They laughed and bellowed and argued, their exuberance infectious.

After dinner, Ugo asked Jonny if he would show him the portrait. Jonny agreed although Emma knew that he would much prefer to show the portrait quietly in the daylight to Ugo alone, without a howling mob in the background.

Emma could tell by the gleam in Jonny's eye that he found this showing of his work a distasteful ordeal but no one would have guessed it from his nonchalant and dégagé air. Her heart was filled with love for him for his pose and his acting and she suddenly realised as she never had before that he was vulnerable.

The picture was set up in a small sitting-room. Jonny fussed about a light for it and eventually managed to fix a reading-lamp to his satisfaction. Emma had helped him unwrap the painting and he now turned to her and said, "Do you think that light is all right?"

"Yes," Emma said. The painting to her seemed simply beautiful. Paola was alive, leaping out of the canvas, but apart from that, there was a wonderful mysterious brooding quality about her, to capture the viewer's imagination, to make him wonder not only at the beauty of the face but on what went on behind the lovely eyes.

"Go and tell Ugo he can come in," Jonny said to Emma, "and try and keep the horde out for a few minutes, for pity's sake."

Emma did as she was bid and Ugo came in alone and saw the picture by himself for about five minutes, but then he came to the door and asked his guests in. He was very excited and Emma knew at once that he loved the painting. The painting was admired too by everyone else, more or less extravagantly, more or less sincerely, but there was no question on the whole that it impressed most people there, and Ugo Grasselli was both proud and delighted that his judgment and faith in Jonny had been vindicated.

Afterwards they sat on the terrace and Ugo enlarged further on his pleasure and delight. Many of the guests left but there was still a little residue left, talking and gossiping gaily. Jonny was the centre of a small admiring group. Emma sat on the fringe of the circle, nursing her drink, silent. She was very tired and longed to go to bed. Perhaps it would be a good idea to excuse herself now and go to her room so that when Jonny finally tore himself away from his fans, she would be asleep, and there would be no awkwardness and no more talk to-night. But somehow even while thinking this, she could not bring herself to move but lay lethargically in her chair listening to the murmur of voices around her.

More guests left and finally, there were only Ugo, Paola, Elena, a couple of Elena's boy friends, Kit, Jonny and herself still sitting and talking in the cool night air.

Ugo got up. "I must go to bed," he said. "I am tired." He looked down at Jonny. "I am very, very pleased with my protégé," he said. "And now, young man, we shall have to see about that exhibition in Rome in the autumn. You are going to have a big success in front of you."

After he had gone, Paola stood up and stretched her arms above her head and yawned and said, "I too am going to bed. I am very tired."

Elena, giggling in a dark corner with her boy friends, turned round at her words. "So early, Paola? Don't go yet."

"I must."

Elena's young men, clearly taking the hint that it was time for them to leave, stood up. There were good nights all round. The moment could no longer be postponed. Emma stood up too and made her good-byes and good nights and went off to their room.

Jonny did not follow her immediately. Paola detained him for a moment in the hall. She caught hold of him by the arm and Emma heard her say, "You see I was right. I am so happy now. About the picture — and about other things, too, I must admit."

Emma heard no more for she walked into the bedroom and closed the door. The maid had done as she had asked and pushed the beds apart. Now a table with a pretty shaded light separated them.

She was in the bathroom cleaning her teeth when Jonny came in. She loitered over her washing still trying to postpone the inevitable moment when they must be really alone together, in the dark, lying side by side.

But at last she had finished and unwillingly she stepped back into the bedroom.

Jonny was in pyjamas, sitting on the edge of a bed, leafing through a magazine, clearly waiting for her to finish. He looked up at her. His dark eyes seemed to blaze with suppressed emotion. He waved his hand at the beds.

"I suppose this tasteful and fastidious rearrangement is what you were gabbing about with the maid?" he said. He smiled at her with derision. "You really do think you're precious, don't you, Emma? And fantastically alluring?" He threw his magazine aside and said savagely, "I wouldn't touch you if I were paid! You're perfectly safe even without the table between us!" He went into the bathroom without another word.

Trembling with unhappiness, Emma undressed quickly, and slipped into her nightie and got into bed. She turned out the light on her side and then lay with her back to Jonny's bed. She wanted to cry bitter tears of rage and mortification. The effort of holding back her sobs was almost more than she could make, but to break down now would make matters ten times worse.

Jonny came back into the room and got into bed. She did not speak and neither did he. Soon his light was off and they were in darkness.

Emma opened her eyes. The room was not wholly dark. Moonlight filtered in through the shutters and soon she could distinguish pieces of furniture. She lay awake for a long time. She heard the occasional sound of a car and the pop-popping of a scooter and once she heard the beat of hoofs and the rumble of cart wheels, and over-laying all these loud noises was the gentle soughing of the trees surrounding the house, mingled with a deeper sound, a muffled sighing. At length, Emma realised that the sighing was the sound of the sea.

She moved gently in her bed, trying to find comfort and sleep. Jonny seemed to have been asleep for a long while. She could hear him breathing, evenly and regularly. He evidently had no tangled emotions to keep him awake.

There were aspirins in the bathroom and a drink of water. Perhaps if she took some aspirin, her turbulent feelings would be quietened and she would be able to get to sleep.

Stealthily she got out of bed and padded across the cool marble floor into the bathroom. Her eyes were accustomed by now to the dark and she found what she wanted without any trouble. She swallowed the aspirin and crept back into the bedroom. For a moment she stood by the window peering between the slats of the shutters into the garden outside. It was a beautiful moonlit night. Gently she pushed the shutters back. They creaked a little and she looked fearfully at Jonny, but he did not stir.

She leaned over the sill and looked down into the garden. Below her there was a flower-bed and the sweet smell of nicotiana rose to greet her. Beyond was the lawn and then a sandy clearing, overhung with trees, where the servants' quarters had been built. Away to the left was the driveway of the house, shining white in the moonlight like a stretch of snow. The sky was very clear and she could see a glimpse of the moon between the trees.

She leant over the sill a long time, drinking the conventional beauty of the night, taking comfort from it, in some strange way. How many times, she wondered, had people looked at the moon in a brilliant sky and found peace from it? For she could feel peace stealing over her heart in gentle waves. There was a gentle breeze and the trees whispered, quiet papery tales, which faded to a sigh. She suddenly heard the crunch of footsteps on the gravel drive and looked to see who was walking abroad at this late hour. Probably one of the servants. But the footsteps came on past the servants' quarters, their owner hidden by the trees. Then they suddenly stopped and a figure appeared on the lawn. It was a girl. Her dress shone white in the moonlight. She walked across the lawn, carefully, skirting the house. It was Paola. Emma almost cried out in amazement. Paola had gone to bed hours ago. It must be at least three o'clock in the morning. Where could she have been at this late hour? She had heard that nobody liked going to bed early in San Carlo and the night-clubs were open till five a.m. but Paola had so specifically stated she was tired.

Paola disappeared round a corner of the house, still walking silently, avoiding the crunchy gravel.

Emma got back into bed, and puzzling over Paola's mysterious past-midnight stroll, soon fell asleep.

In the morning when she awoke, the room was flooded with sunlight, and her miseries of the night before seemed like a nightmare, and the mystery of Paola in the moonlit garden something else she had dreamed up.

Jonny's bed was empty and he was not in the bathroom. He had evidently awakened early after his sweet untroubled sleep.

The maid came in while she was lying there ruminating. She had brought Emma's breakfast and a message from *il signore*. Jonny had gone down to the beach.

Later when Emma had breakfasted and was dressing, Elena appeared.

"You are almost as bad as an Italian at getting up," Elena smiled. "Jonny and Kit were very British and rushed off for a swim at some terribly early hour. At least nine."

Emma laughed. "What time is it now? My watch has stopped." She was astonished to see that it was nearly eleven. She must have overslept after her wakefulness in the night.

"A civilised hour. Hurry up and I will wait for you," said Elena, who was looking very pretty in white shorts and a lemon coloured blouse and flat gold sandals.

"Where is Paola?" asked Emma, pulling on her tapered purple pants.

"She went off to the beach too very early," said Elena. "Paola is up to something, do you know that?" She looked mysterious for a moment. "I have my suspicions," she added darkly. "Paola is not as good as she pretends to my uncle."

Emma put on the vividly patterned silk blouse she had bought to go with the pants in Florence, and following Elena's example she also wore her gold sandals.

"You look very nice," remarked Elena. "I love that blouse. It suits you."

When Emma arrived on the beach, she did indeed find that her bright and gay clothes blended perfectly with their background. Elena led her across the smooth sands to the Grasselli family awning where Ugo was already sitting, reading his papers. Kit and Jonny were sprawled on the sand, basking in the sun.

Kit sat up when he saw them. "Hallo, there," he said, welcome in his voice, "here come the lazy lie-abeds. You both look good enough to eat," he added. Emma smiled at him, her eyes veiled with sun-glasses. She glanced at Jonny but he too was wearing dark glasses and she could not tell whether he was looking at her or at Elena.

"Let's go and change," said Elena, "I am longing to go in the water."

"I have no bathing-suit," Emma said. "I did not come equipped for a beach holiday."

"Oh there are dozens of bathing-suits in the *cabina*," said Elena generously. "You can borrow one of mine or Paola's. I am sure they would fit you."

In the *cabina* with Elena, Emma saw why Elena had been so sure she would find something to fit her. The 'suits' were all bikinis, mere wisps of material. Emma preferred less flamboyant wear for sea bathing and she tied on the scarlet bikini, which Elena handed her, with some misgiving. However she was slim enough to wear it. But she planned to go shopping as soon as she could and buy an ordinary swim-suit.

Jonny's eyes were on her, she knew, as she came out of the *cabina* and rejoined the others under the awning. But she would not look at him. She felt self-conscious and thought, 'I suppose he is disapproving as usual and thinks I am play-acting again. Well, I don't care!' But, of course, she knew in her heart, that she did care. She wanted Jonny's approval more than anything in the world, and one compliment from him would be worth more to her than a thousand pressed on her by Kit Sundine.

"I'm going for a swim," said Elena directly. She pulled a cap over her hair and ran off down to the sea.

"What about you?" asked Kit of Emma.

Emma sat down on the hot sand and Kit rolled over so that he faced her. He offered her a cigarette and then leant forward with his lighter.

Emma puffed at her cigarette for a moment. She could feel Kit's eyes staring at her and turned to meet his gaze.

"Yes?" she said questioningly.

"I said nothing."

"No, but you were thinking something," Emma said.

"Only that," Kit lowered his voice a little, "you are looking marvellous, no longer a naiad but a mermaid."

"Oh, Kit," Emma laughed spontaneously at his extravagance. "I think you must lie awake thinking these things up."

"How about a swim?" Kit asked. He turned to Jonny who was lying a few yards away, his head propped up on a cushion, reading a book.

"I'll go later," Jonny murmured without looking up from his page.

"Come on then," Kit said to Emma.

They walked towards the sea. Emma's slim body looked pale in contrast to Kit's bronze tan. As they neared the water Kit said, "Do you want a proper swim?" Emma looked at him, puzzled.

"The water is very shallow," Kit explained, "but if we take a *patino* out, we can row to where it's deeper and dive. Would you like that?"

"Very much," Emma said.

Kit called to one of the beach boys, and together they pushed a *patino* into the water. A *patino*, Emma was to discover, was simply two pontoons fixed together with crossways planks fitted with seats for the oarsman and passengers. She sat on the seat opposite Kit who took the two big oars.

The sea was very calm and a beautiful milky green. In a minute or so they were beyond the little, gentle frilly waves which edged the beach and were among the children in their rubber boats, the sunbathers on their airfilled mattresses. Kit rowed on until they were a good way from the shore. They were out of their depth now and there were fewer swimmers. The calm glassy sea was dotted with all kinds of craft, many *patini*, little sailing yachts, the occasional motor vessel. The bright umbrellas on the beach looked like so much brilliant confetti and the cries of the children were faint and disembodied, floating across the water.

Behind the beach, there were dark green pine woods and away off to the right, white against the intense blue sky, there was the peaky outline of the mountains. It was incredibly tranquil and peaceful. The beauty of it all seemed to underline Emma's deep unhappiness. She had been controlling her memory all morning, refusing to dwell on Jonny's words of the night before, trying to be beguiled and made forgetful by the scene and the people around her.

But now the very scene itself seemed to torment her. How happy she could be in this place if — if — if. If. A horrible word. If only Jonny were kind and loving to her. If he were in love with her. If only he were like he used to be, friendly and funny. But he had turned into a cruel man who hated her. Now the memory of the night before, his cutting words, came pouring into her mind.

Kit, who had been silent while rowing, wrapped in his own thoughts, rested on his oars and looked down into the water. It was clear and deep.

"How will this do?" he asked Emma. He shipped his oars and then cut into the water, a slim brown streak. He seemed to be under for ages and then his head appeared some yards away and he turned round, laughing, and shook the hair out of his eyes.

Emma dived after him. She loved swimming and she had a graceful style though perhaps she was not a very powerful swimmer.

They swam and dived for some time. Emma swooped in and out of the water with a quiet desperation. Only think of this moment. The slippery edge of the *patino*, the dark green water, the sudden immersion, then up into the air again. Shake your hair out of your eyes, swim back, climb on to the *patino* again. Don't think of Jonny. She tired before Kit. She climbed back on to the *patino* and caught hold of the oars and rowed a little and gently drifted, exhausted, but her thoughts still beating like a hammer in her brain. 'You really do think you're precious!' 'Fantastically alluring!' '*I wouldn't touch you if I were paid!*'

Kit caught hold of one end of the *patino* pointed upwards like the toe of an Eastern slipper. He trod water for a while, grinning up at her.

"Hey," he said, "you're so quiet. Have you gone to sleep?"

Emma shook herself out of her reverie

and put her hand like a comb through her wet tangled hair.

"Where is Paola this morning?" she asked. "I haven't seen her."

"Oh, about her affairs, I suppose," said Kit. He heaved himself up and the *patino* rocked with his added weight.

"She's very determined, Paola, you know, Emma," he said as he took up the oars again. "Especially when she's set on something as she is now."

Emma glanced down into the water. Were these words a warning to her?

"You know about it?" Kit asked. Emma nodded without looking at him.

"Ugo is not going to be so easy to persuade," said Kit, beginning to row for the shore. "Paola has a long hard haul in front of her."

"Don't you have any sympathy — I mean don't you think it's awful?" Emma burst out, anguished by his calm acceptance of her crumbling world.

Kit looked at her in surprise. "It's pretty rough, I suppose, but mainly very stupid," he said. "In any case, it's futile to think a clandestine affair remains clandestine. Somebody always tumbles to it in the end. I guessed about this thing long before Paola told me."

Emma said nothing more. She was too proud to confide her own feelings to Kit. Presumably Paola had told him everything. Jonny must surely have told her the reason for their marriage, that it was no marriage at all, except legally.

# 10

IN the evening, Paola suggested that they went to a sea food restaurant down by the harbour farther down the coast for dinner. In the end, there was quite a party of them, Emma and Jonny, Paola and Kit, Elena and three other young men. The place was crowded but Paola had booked a table and they were conducted with a flourish to a very good one near the window. The walls of the restaurant were decorated with seascape paintings by local artists and hung with fishing-nets, the waiters were dressed in red and white striped shirts and pale blue pants and an enormous variety of fish and shell-fish was laid out on a marble slab in the entrance for their choice and delectation.

Their dinner when it arrived lived up to the promise of the décor.

The night was intensely hot and stifling but a breeze came in through the open window and Emma who was nearest to it could look out across the harbour. Below them was a narrow strip of sand reflected in the lights from the restaurant and then, beyond, the water, twinkling with lights from the fishing-smacks and pleasure yachts at anchor.

Kit was sitting beside Emma, Jonny was opposite her. She had not seen much of him all afternoon. He had insisted that Paola give him one more sitting, much to her annoyance, but with her father's help, Jonny had won the day.

"Everyone thinks the portrait is perfect," Paola sulked. "Why do you still want to go on fiddling with it?"

"For me it is not quite finished," Jonny had turned to Ugo Grasselli, "and I cannot bear to leave it like this." So Paola and Jonny had spent most of the afternoon together closeted in the small sitting-room. Emma had not seen the portrait again but she had heard Ugo exclaiming about it just before they left for the restaurant. She was happy for Jonny that his patron was so pleased, and she wondered if Jonny had yet written to Professor Maxwell Graham, his teacher in London who had set in motion this sojourn in Italy and who had always been such a believer in his talent.

She asked him now, looking directly across the table at him: "Have you written to Professor Graham?"

Jonny stared at her, his eyes cold. "No," he said briefly. "There's time enough for that." He turned away and began talking to Elena who was sitting on one side of him with Paola on the other.

Emma felt snubbed. She thought, 'He shuts me right out of everything.' She felt tears sting her eyelids and looked down at her food. She felt completely alone. She did not speak much for the rest of the meal but no one seemed to notice her silence. The others, including Jonny, all seemed very gay and at the end, when a huge basket of fruit was brought to finish their meal, Paola said, "You know we are all going to Nino's afterwards to dance? Don't you think that is a good idea?"

"You must excuse me," Emma said quickly, "I have a headache. I don't think I shall be able to come." A hot stuffy night-club was the last place in which she wanted to find herself.

"Oh but you must come," Paola pleaded. "Nino's is always very gay. You will enjoy it. It is right by the sea front and it is always cool."

Emma protested once more and then left it. Perhaps she would be able to persuade Kit to run her home while the others went on to Nino's. When they were waiting outside the restaurant, arranging who was to go in what car, she broached the subject to Kit quietly. But he answered her emphatically, "You've got to come, Emma. It will buck you up. I know you're down in the dumps, but you can't go home alone. I won't take you anyway. You will enjoy yourself when you get there."

Nino's turned out to be a long low ranch-type building with verandas all round. As Paola had said, it was right by the sea and the customers could sit on the veranda and look out over the sands and hear the sea whispering in the darkness in front of them.

The place was crowded. There were many pretty women around and a rumty-tumty band. Paola was greeted by the owner and they were all seated at another good table on the veranda. Emma felt she was moving around from place to place like some sort of ghost. It did not matter what her surroundings were. She felt only pain and a kind of physical sickness. She thought how stupid the old cure-all of a change of scene was. A change of scene did not mean a change of heart.

Jonny asked her to dance immediately and she got up mechanically and followed him on to the dance floor.

They danced in silence for a few moments, moving rhythmically together. There was something almost hypnotic about the music, Emma felt, and for a few moments all thought was suspended and she was only conscious of the moment, the golden lights of the night-club, the smoky scented atmosphere, the feel of Jonny's arms around her and the throb and beat of the band. It was Jonny who broke their silence, "Heaven knows what we are doing in this place," he said, breaking her trance. "Or perhaps you are enjoying it?"

"I didn't want to come in the first place," Emma pointed out, "but now that I am here it is not so bad."

"Ah," Jonny whispered softly, "but you were persuaded by Kit. You find his blandishments hard to resist, Emma. Is he so very attractive to you?" Emma was silent but Jonny persisted, "Do you think he is attractive?"

"Yes, I do," Emma admitted.

"And you are in love with him?" He held her away from him and looked down into her eyes.

"I suppose you think it would be very convenient if I were?" Emma countered sharply.

"Convenient? That's a funny word to choose. Are you in love with him, Emma? You haven't answered my question."

"Just because I say I think he's attractive, it doesn't mean I am in love with him," Emma said. "The world — this night-club — is full of attractive men but I don't go round falling in love with them all."

"Is Kit in love with you?"

"Not that I know of. He's not in love with anyone."

"He pays you a great deal of attention," Jonny said with an edge to his voice.

"I think he likes me," said Emma. "I

think he finds me attractive. Is that so very unusual? Not everyone is like you, Jonny. But he is not in love with me. So you see your happy little solution won't work."

"What happy little solution?"

"Pairing me off with Kit."

"That's the last thing I have ever wanted to do."

The music had stopped and he took her back to their table. But before she could sit down, Kit arose and took her back on to the floor again. As he steered her down one side of the long room, he said, "Have you seen Paola's lover yet?" He nodded towards the band.

The band was large and all the young men in it had crew-cut hair, wore white pants and red and white striped blazers. They were very lively.

Emma, not understanding Kit, looked at them in puzzlement. "The pianist, silly," Kit said. Emma glanced at the pianist. His face was familiar to her and she suddenly realised it was the same young man to whom Paola had introduced her all those weeks ago at the Caravella in Florence. The young man who had played the piano in the café-bar and whom Paola had asked her not to mention at home. "My father is *très snob*," she had said.

"Signor Valli," Emma said.

"Have you met him?" Kit asked.

"Once, a long time ago, when we first arrived," Emma said.

"How long have you known about it?" Kit asked. "I mean when did Paola take you into her confidence? I only found out by accident."

"I am not in Paola's confidence," Emma said hesitantly.

Kit glanced down at her. "I thought you knew all about it," he said, in surprise. "You told me you did this morning."

"Paola told me she was in love," whispered Emma, "but she did not say with whom. I thought it was someone else."

"Who did you think it was, for heaven's sake? Me?"

Emma shook her head. "She and Jonny have been so close," she said and faltered, "I thought, I thought it was Jonny."

Kit almost stopped dancing in amazement, and then he recovered himself and guided her to the edge of the floor. He looked down at her concerned. "Are you all right, Emma? You look very pale all of a sudden. Let's go to the bar and I'll buy you a drink."

"I don't want a drink," Emma said. "Let me get some fresh air."

They got off the dance floor and Kit took hold of her arm and led her on to the veranda. For a moment they leaned in silence over its railing and then Kit said, "Would you like to go for a walk? We can get down on the sands from here. There are some steps."

Emma followed where he led and in a few moments they were walking along the sand, now swept smooth for the morning by the beach boys. The umbrellas and awnings were sheathed and folded away and their skeletons looked ghostly in the light shining out from the restaurant.

Kit slipped his arm through Emma's. "Why should you think Paola was in love with Jonny?" he asked. "I know that she has had a kind of hero worship for him and obviously thinks he is very attractive, but just because she thinks a man attractive does not mean she is in love with him." There was an echo of familiarity about his words and Emma realised that he was repeating almost word for word what she had said earlier on to Jonny about their two selves.

She said miserably, "But I've seen Jonny and Paola together — when they didn't know — "

Kit stopped in his tracks, "Uh-huh!" he said. "Just what exactly has been going on under my nose and I haven't noticed it?" he asked. "I know Paola is a minx but I wouldn't have thought she would run two men at the same time — and one of them married, at that." He paused and then added, "And yet, on second thoughts, I suppose she might think it clever to play one off against the other. What about Jonny? Does he know about Arturo Valli?"

"I don't know," said Emma. "I don't know anything. I have had to guess everything. Jonny has not told me about Paola but I think he wants to now — I think that is why we came here this week-end."

"Paola came here this week-end," said Kit grimly, "because Arturo Valli left Florence to join the band at Nino's, and the band at Nino's is going to the U.S. in a couple of days and Arturo is going with it."

"I see," said Emma. "Is Arturo Valli the same young man — the music master — about whom there was a fuss last year?"

"So you heard about that? From Elena, I'd like to bet. Yes, it's the same man. He disappeared from Florence for a time, and then he turned up again and Paola, apparently, found she hadn't got over him. I only knew she was seeing him again when I met them one afternoon in Florence by accident. I am afraid I felt rather responsible about it and I wanted to phone Uncle Ugo and tell him but Paola persuaded me not to. Then, just before we came to San Carlo, Paola and Arturo had a terrible row, but I managed to straighten that out. It was mainly I think because Arturo was planning to slip quietly away to America and out of Paola's life for good. I really began to believe they were truly in love, but now that I hear about Jonny, I wonder. Emma dear, what are you going to do?"

"I don't know," Emma said unhappily. "You were right about our marriage, Kit. Jonny and I only got married for the sake of the prize. At least that was why he married me" — a sob escaped her involuntarily — "but I have been in love with him for years. It's just one of those things."

"Ah, my poor darling," Kit said and put his arm round her shoulders. His tone was soft and sympathetic and Emma knew that she had his sympathy but not his understanding. He did not know what it was like to love someone so desperately, to want to share another person's life utterly, to want to forgive him even when he had done you harm, to need him like an arm or an eye, because to be with him meant living itself was more vital and varied, with more savour. Food tasted better when she was eating it with Jonny, and a sunset was more beautiful, and even reading a book when he was near was more stimulating.

"Let's go back," Emma said and they both turned and retraced their steps across the soft cool sand.

"Did you have a pleasant walk?" Jonny said, when they rejoined the table.

"How did you know we went for a walk?" Emma asked him, staring at him with a mixture of feelings.

"I saw you leave," Jonny said evenly. It was almost as if he minded, thought Emma wonderingly, as though there was a return of the jealousy he had displayed the night of the *palio*. He did not ask her to dance again and she sat looking at the floor, watching people whirl by unseeingly. The news which Kit had imparted had astonished her, but the more she thought it over, the more it explained Paola's movements of the past few weeks — the constant jaunts into Florence when she, Emma, had thought she was with Jonny, last night in the garden, the sudden rush to San Carlo. Emma wondered if Jonny were completely in the dark about Arturo Valli, if he had ever met him. Her question was answered in a little while when Arturo came and joined them, and Paola introduced him all round. He stayed with them for about an hour, evidently having some time off from his musical duties.

He was silent and unsmiling and after being introduced to them, addressed all his infrequent remarks to Paola. He did not appear madly in love with her, Emma thought, only now and again allowing his gaze to rest on her, darkly and inscrutably.

Elena pointedly ignored him and talked only with Jonny and Kit and the other young men in their party. Clearly she disapproved of him completely.

Paola was defensively gay and vivacious, pretending not to notice Elena's behaviour. She chattered all the time, in both Italian and English, translating everyone's remarks for Arturo's benefit, trying to draw him into their circle.

Once she turned to Emma and cried, "You must speak in Italian now. Arturo is shy and besides, he has very little English."

So Emma did her best and exchanged a few polite phrases with Arturo who seemed to her more surly than shy.

Later Paola cried, looking across the table at him and at Jonny — they were sitting side by side — "Do you know you two are very much alike!"

Jonny looked guardedly at Arturo, who returned the look equally warily. Paola repeated her remark in Italian to him.

They were a bit alike, Emma admitted to herself. Both were good-looking in a dark, wild sort of way, with thick black hair and they were both well built and lithe and quick in their movements. Yet to her, there seemed such a vast difference in their personalities that it cancelled out any mere physical resemblance. The one's sombre exterior seemed merely a mask for somnolence and indifference while Jonny seemed to burn with an unquenchable fiery spirit. But perhaps, thought Emma, there were banked fires of feeling in Arturo. Only Paola would know. She caught Jonny looking at her. "Isn't it time we went home?" he said. He sounded inexpressibly weary.

Emma was suddenly filled with pity for him. Perhaps the existence of Arturo Valli, perhaps Paola's obvious pre-occupation with him, had been a shock for him. Just how much did Jonny care for Paola?

"I'm perfectly ready to go home," she said.

"So are we all," said Kit, "except possibly Paola." He looked at his cousin questioningly.

"Oh, I'm ready too," Paola said, gazing across the dance floor to the bandstand where Arturo Valli had taken possession of the piano again.

They came out of the night-club into the clear freshness of a starlit night. I will think of everything to-morrow, Emma promised herself, as they skimmed back to the house in Kit's car. She felt exhausted with emotion.

# 11

JONNY hardly spoke to her as they made their preparations for sleep. He seemed morose and thoughtful and stood by the window a long time before getting into bed, looking out into the garden, and smoking a last cigarette.

Emma was a long time getting to sleep and this night she was conscious that Jonny too was lying wakeful in the other bed, not moving but lying still and quiet as she was. And thinking what? Possibly his thoughts were at least as painful as hers.

In the morning, he shared her breakfast which the maid brought in about nine. He sat on the edge of his bed while Emma sat up in hers, the controversial table between them with the tray laid upon it. His hair was ruffled and untidy, and his face dark with stubble and yet in his pink and white pyjamas, there was something of a little boy about him. He looks about eight, thought Emma, a little boy who's had a bad dream, and she longed to pull his head to her breast and cradle him and rock him into happiness and contentment. He yawned unselfconsciously and passed his hand across his chin, feeling its roughness.

He looked across the table at Emma, his eyes bold and exploring, studying her face, her hair, the bare shoulders above her nightgown without any pretence. His scrutiny bothered Emma.

"I hope you slept well," she said politely.

"I had a lousy night," Jonny said unequivocally.

"Oh," said Emma, "I'm sorry."

"I don't think you give a damn," said Jonny equably, "stop pretending, Emma. I think I can stand anything except dishonesty. What do you want to do this morning?"

"I want to buy a swim-suit," Emma said, disconcerted. "I think it is worth it even for a day or so more. Paola and Elena only have bikinis."

"You looked very nice in your bikini yesterday," Jonny said.

"Your figure is as beautiful as any on

the beach. In fact," he added slowly, "you're a beautiful creature altogether. You seem to have blossomed in the sun."

Emma felt herself flushing at his words and busied herself with the coffee cups. "You're very complimentary this morning," she murmured.

"I brought an English rose-bud to Italy," Jonny went on, a teasing note in his voice, "and she's blossomed into a gaudy passion flower."

"I misunderstood you," Emma said quietly. "I see you were sneering at me."

"Sneering at you!" Jonny said in mock horror. "Never let it be said! I'm sweet talking you, Emma. I happen to like passion flowers. I find my taste being cultivated that way." He sighed a little. "We can't spend all our time fighting," he said, "or can we?"

Emma looked up to meet his eyes, fixed on her questioningly, almost, she thought with a little tremor of the heart, pleadingly. "I have never wanted to fight," she said slowly.

Jonny gave a short derisive laugh. "Not

much," he said. "Give me another cup of coffee. I'll come with you and help choose the new swim-suit," he added surprisingly.

San Carlo had many little *boutiques* and small dress shops to tempt and trap the holiday maker. Jonny and Emma wandered around for a little while exploring the town. And then Jonny's eye was caught by a whole windowful of swim wear, bikinis, classically cut swim-suits, frilly play-suits.

"This is obviously the shop with the mostest," he said.

Emma looked at the array. She pointed to a little pile of baby pink and baby blue suits. "I suppose you think I should go for those," she said a little slyly.

Jonny shook his head. "I prefer that one," he said and pointed to a plain white suit scattered all over with deep red poppies. "Or even that one," he added, picking out another in wonderfully fiery colours in a splashy all-over pattern. "I've given in, Emma. I've admitted you're right. I like you in bright colours."

Afterwards, when they had bought the poppy suit, he suggested they have a swim before lunch and then she could wear it.

The beach was crowded but there was no one under the Grasselli awning.

"Maybe they are all bathing," suggested Emma. She was happier than she had been for weeks past. In fact, she was so happy that she did not dare stop and think about it. For once, she and Jonny had been relaxed together, as though they had both come to terms with the devil which had been besetting them.

'Perhaps I am getting resigned,' Emma thought as she undressed in the *cabina* and put on her new suit, 'resigned to being second best. Perhaps Jonny is resigned too — to losing Paola.'

He had been so kind this morning. The cold, cruel Jonny who had said such cutting things had disappeared and the old Jonny had come back, the gay, warm Jonny of four years ago.

They swam far out until they came to deep water. The sea was full of small lumps of seaweed which Jonny threw at her playfully. They dived like porpoises and then they swam back, and walked dripping up the beach, tired but refreshed.

When they arrived back at 'Il Cappannello della Nonna,' they found the others having an apéritif before lunch on the terrace. Kit and Elena had gone for a sail early in the morning and had only just got back, Ugo had been busy with business. Only Paola did not vouchsafe what she had been doing. Apparently she had just come in before Emma and Jonny.

"And where have you been?" Ugo asked her. His voice was curiously significant.

"Oh, I went shopping too," Paola said quickly, "with Jonny and Emma."

"How odd," said Ugo Grasselli, another edge to his voice, "for I was told you had been seen water ski-ing with Arturo Valli."

Paola looked at him with bright eyes and then glanced at her cousin Elena. "And who told you that?" she asked.

"It does not matter who told me," said Ugo. He looked at Jonny. "Did Paola come with you?" and while Jonny hesitated, he turned to Emma: "So Paola

302

was with you?" In the silence while Emma tried to think of something to say which was not a direct lie, Paola said with bravado: "All right, I was with Arturo Valli. I happened to bump into him this morning."

"I have also been told that you have been seeing him in Florence," Ugo went on.

At this, Paola flashed a look of murderous hatred at Kit. "Kit, you promised me — you promised me — "

Kit raised his hands. "This is nothing to do with me," he protested. "I know nothing about it."

"Well, then, it is Elena," Paola cried, staring at her other cousin.

"Have you been seeing Valli in Florence while I have been down here?" demanded her father.

Paola stood up and said defiantly, "Yes, I have. He was why I stayed in Florence in the first place. I have seen him every day since you went away. I intend to go on seeing him every day for the rest of my life. He is leaving for America the day after to-morrow. I am going with him. We're going to get married as soon as we get to New York."

There was complete and utter silence for a few moments when she had finished, and then Ugo Grasselli rose to his feet.

"You are embarrassing our guests, Paola," he said, "we will discuss your plans after lunch."

"I am not embarrassing our guests," cried Paola, "I want everyone to know. It's official." She broke into a sudden flood of Italian and was answered by her father also in his own language and then he excused himself to the others in English.

"I am sorry to inflict this family quarrel on you," he said. "Paola is talking nonsense, of course."

"I am not talking nonsense," Paola stamped her foot. The argument between them rose in force. The others all stood up and unobtrusively wandered off. One of the servants appeared and announced that lunch was ready but no one took any notice of him.

Emma and Jonny went to their room.

"You know," said Jonny thoughtfully, "I always had my suspicions that Paola had assignations in Florence."

There was a knock at the door and Kit put his head round. "I thought you might be in here," he said. He held a telegram in his hand. "I've just heard that I've got to go back to Rome. The studio want me. It's a bit of a bore but on the other hand with all this fuss going on, maybe it's a good idea. I think perhaps we'd better have our lunch. If anyone is hungry?"

The three of them went into the dining-room and were joined by Elena, and later still by Paola. Ugo Grasselli did not appear.

Paola looked fierce and unrepentant. "Oh, I expect he's rushing round trying to put a spoke in my plans," she said, "but he can't and he won't. I shall make a big scandal. I have bought my air-line ticket. He cannot lock me up, and if he has me dragged off the plane just think what a lovely treat that will be for all the newspapers. I shall threaten to sell my story to a magazine. I am not going to be parted from Arturo again. It was fate which brought us together for the second time. If he goes to America, I may never see him again."

"You are not very practical," Elena observed. "He has no money and a funny sort of job."

"His present job is a very good one," Paola flashed, "and do not think that I will forget that you told my father, Elena."

Elena shrugged. "Someone would have told him sooner or later," she said.

"I would have got away quietly," said Paola, "now it will be more difficult, but I shall succeed." She looked across at Emma. "And to think that if I had not gone shopping with you that afternoon, if we had not gone to the skirt shop, I would not have met Bianca Giovanni and I would not have known that Arturo was back in Florence. He thought I was in San Carlo, you see. If Jonny had not come to Florence, if my father had not wanted me painted, I would have been in San Carlo. You see how everything hangs on a thread." She helped herself to salad and went on talking as though longing to unburden herself of all her secrets.

"And then the painting lessons, and the portrait — they made such a wonderful excuse to stay in Florence and be near Arturo while he was playing at the Caravella. I could not see him at night because of his job but of course I could see him every afternoon. Emma and Jonny were always out in the afternoons, Jonny always wanted to go into Florence. It was perfect, and then some days, Arturo and I would come back to the villa. We had it entirely to ourselves. It was blissful."

Emma looked up from her plate, a sudden shaft of hope and understanding piercing her heart. "Did you go sometimes to the studio?" she asked.

Paola looked a little shamefaced. "Well, yes, we did," she said. "You see, in the house, there were servants and I did not particularly want the servants to know about Arturo so when you were not there, we stayed in the studio. It was not perhaps very nice when you were our guests and it was your home, as it were, but I knew also that if you knew about it, you would understand and not mind."

"No," said Emma, her mind racing on. And I came back one afternoon early and saw you and *Arturo* embracing, and thought it was Jonny. And I saw you and Arturo another time going into the house when I was in the garden, and I thought Jonny had changed his shirt. She looked at Jonny. Could she have been so mad as to have mistaken him for Arturo? But it was possible. They were alike. Other people had said so, and the light in the studio had been dim and aqueous, shadowy because the blinds were down against the sun. And she had not stayed. She had seen a dark head, a back which looked like Jonny's back. She had not known about Arturo. She had jumped to a wild conclusion and run away. If she had gone into that room, how much heart-break she would have prevented. And once the seed was planted in her head, her jealousy of Paola, of her beauty and talent had done the rest.

Emma felt humbled. She had been vile and she had done Jonny a horrible injustice. And yet, and yet, he had liked Paola. He had thought her beautiful and had painted her with love. And yet even as she thought this, Emma also realised that he could perhaps have liked her no more than she liked Kit. And naturally he was moved by her beauty, as she, Emma, had been. Jonny was an artist besides. Beauty, rare beauty, or the beauty he often saw in everyday objects, he wanted to capture, to translate into paint on canvas. All his life, beautiful women would come to him for their portraits and the only way he would want to possess them would be in paint. Their skin tones would mean no more to him than Chinese white with a touch of ochre, of crimson lake, the lights on their hair, chrome yellow or burnt umber.

"Paola," Kit said, "what has your father got against Arturo? Is it that his birth is humble or his job insecure? I know Arturo Valli is a good man, but no father wants his daughter to marry a man with an insecure future. Have you ever discussed this thing calmly with your father?"

"He knows Arturo," Paola said sullenly. "He himself employed him in the first place. I think he liked him then but afterwards he felt Arturo had been ungrateful to fall in love with his only daughter."

"His *rich* only daughter," said Kit

gently. "If you like, I will go to your father and tell him that Arturo was going to leave you, run away from you, because that would be best for you, that I don't think he wants to marry you because you are wealthy but because he loves you."

Sudden tears sprang into Paola's eyes and she dashed them away hurriedly with her hand. She looked at Jonny and Emma. "I am sorry to be so silly," she said and ran out of the room.

Emma put down her knife and fork. She could not finish her lunch. She felt sick with mingled self-abasement and self-hate.

They all rose from the table and Kit looking at his watch said, "I'm going to pack. I'll try and see Uncle Ugo later, but I must leave for Rome to-night."

Emma went to her room. Somehow she must make amends to Jonny for her silent accusations, for her lack of trust in him. Somehow she must explain her behaviour to him. Oh they had started out on the wrong foot all right. He had been practical and uncomplimentary but it was her suspicions of him which had made their situation worse than ever.

Jonny came into the bedroom. He shut the door carefully behind him.

"Emma, let's go back to Florence," he said. "I have just been talking to Kit. He is willing to drive us there. It is out of his way but not all that much, and he says he does not mind. With all this family hoo-ha going on, I think we would be better out of it. What do you think? If we leave this evening, we will be there not too late to-night. Kit might spend the night at the villa or he might drive on and get to Rome early to-morrow morning."

"I would like to go back," Emma said quickly. "I am sure Ugo Grasselli will be glad to be rid of us."

"Good, good," Jonny said. "Anyway, you start packing and I will see if I can find Ugo and explain what we intend doing."

# 12

AS Jonny had expected, Ugo Grasselli, though he politely tried to hide it, was obviously pleased that his house guests had chosen to depart.

Kit and Jonny and Emma left 'Il Cappannello della Nonna' in the early evening. After the storms of the afternoon, and much coming and going, the atmosphere was comparatively calm and Kit was optimistic about a reconciliation between Paola and her father. When they left, Arturo Valli was expected on a visit at any minute. Paola was still as determined as ever to marry him, but now her father, after Kit's special pleading, was beginning to weaken.

"Arturo himself will do the trick," said Kit confidently, as they drove away. "He is sensible and his present contract is a very good one. It is a very good band and they are going to have a very good tour with good money and prospects of a big success. Nobody wants a jazz pianist for a son-in-law from choice probably, but a successful one and perhaps a famous one is something else again. Arturo is very good."

"I will write to you from America," Paola had promised both Jonny and Emma, showing that she still meant to get her own way. She gave her *maestro*, as she called him affectionately for the last time, a big bear-like hug, and as she watched the embrace, Emma saw it for what it was, a warm parting between friends. Paola hugged her too. "You have been my lucky mascot," she whispered.

"I wish you a million times more luck," Emma answered, feeling contrite, "and all the happiness in the world."

Kit drove fast and furiously. None of them spoke much on the journey back to Florence. Emma was busy with her own troubled, self-chastising thoughts, Kit clearly was thinking now only of the work awaiting him in Rome and his horses, and Jonny brooded, his face closed up and secretive.

"You must come up to Rome," Kit said absently once. "I'll show you round, and you must see some of the chariot races we've been rehearsing. They're really pretty good."

He made excellent time and almost before she thought it could be possible, they were cruising up the long drive of the Grasselli villa. There were a few lights to welcome them and Mario came out as soon as he saw the car and helped to unload their bags. Ugo Grasselli had already phoned to warn him of their arrival.

"I think I shall press on," said Kit. "I don't feel tired and I am anxious to be back."

They made their farewells. "I shall expect to see you in Rome before long," Kit said and gave Emma a big kiss on both cheeks and a squeeze. Emma followed him to the car.

"Kit," she said, "I must tell you — I was wrong about Jonny and Paola."

Kit put his hands on the wheel. "I thought perhaps you might be," he said.

"It was Arturo and Paola I saw in the studio," Emma explained hurriedly, "I'm sure it was. I've been a fool, Kit."

"Well, stop being a fool," advised Kit.

He nodded in the direction of Jonny who was following Mario down the path to the studio. "You've got a very fine husband there. Repair your fences, Emma."

He pressed the self-starter and flashily turned the car round and swept off down the drive. In a kind of trance, Emma watched his tail-light disappear out of sight and then she ran after Jonny.

Mario had switched on all the lights to welcome them and the studio looked swept and inviting. It was such a short time since they had been away and yet Emma felt she had lived a lifetime. She looked round the studio with pleasure. It seemed wonderfully dear and familiar.

"It's just like home," she said with pleasure.

Jonny glanced at her. "I was thinking the same thing," he said. "Mario wants to know if we want anything to eat, Emma."

"We haven't had any dinner," Emma said. She turned to the servant: "Would you bring us something over, Mario? Soup? Spaghetti?"

When the man had gone Jonny looked at his watch. It was ten o'clock. "Nice for us that servants don't keep union hours in Italy," he said.

"Lovely," said Emma, "but then they do have a sleep in the afternoons."

"They still work too hard," Jonny said. He began walking about the room looking at the pictures on his two easels, on the walls, rearranging small ornaments on the tables. Emma sensed he was nervous, as she was herself.

"Don't make me feel guilty," she said. "I'm hungry."

"So am I," Jonny laughed.

And guilty for ever, thought Emma. She was trying to gird herself to say something to Jonny, to haul down a flag of pride. "Jonny," she began.

At her tone he turned and looked at her questioningly.

"I think I'll go and have a bath," Emma said lamely.

Later when she came down in her candy-striped housecoat she found Jonny sprawled out on the couch. The table for their dinner was all set with a bright checkered cloth, candles, and a flat bowl of gardenias.

Jonny who was still dressed and had

not changed swung his legs off the couch. He yawned, "I fell asleep," he said.

"The table looks very pretty," Emma said.

"A table for two, very romantic," Jonny said. He yawned again.

Emma moved about the studio. She rearranged the flowers at the far end which Mario had squashed in a vase almost up to their necks.

"Jonny," she said.

"Yes, Emma."

"I feel I must tell you something which is on my conscience — I mean you must have thought I've behaved very oddly sometimes — "

"Not to worry," Jonny said blandly, "I'm used to your oddness. In any case, I've made up my mind how to treat you. I'm going to seduce you — with words. I thought, 'Why get het up about Kit Sundine? I can think up as many flowery compliments as he can if that's what she wants.' Softly, softly, catchee monkey. Perhaps I shouldn't tell you, but it's just a fair warning."

Emma pulled out the flower heads with quick nervous gestures. "I don't want flowery compliments," she said.

"Come over here and tell me what you do want. What's on your conscience? Kit Sundine's kisses?"

"Oh," Emma made a sound of exasperation, "Kit Sundine's nothing to me."

"Well, then, why did you watch him out of sight so fondly?" demanded Jonny, "as though you couldn't bear to see him go? Last night, at that Nino place, you were walking with him by the sea for half an hour. Don't tell me you were just walking up and down holding hands!"

"Arm-in-arm," corrected Emma. She leaned against the table. "Jonny, you are making this so difficult for me — and yet I must say it. It's nothing to do with Kit. You and I haven't been friends ever since we came to Italy — and I know I have been partly to blame. But I have thought you were deceiving me with Paola — I was terribly jealous of her from the start — so lovely and so talented. I thought you were in love with her. I could not bear the humiliation. Then one afternoon when I came back early I saw you together in the studio.

318

You were kissing her — "

"Emma, are you stark, raving mad? I've never kissed Paola in my life — " Jonny leapt up from the couch.

"It was Arturo. I thought it was you," Emma said. "And then later you pretended, as I thought, that you had been in Florence. I thought you were lying. Now I know it was the truth."

Jonny sank back on the couch. "You really have a very low opinion of me, haven't you, Emma?" He spoke wryly. "I told you that the promise I made at our marriage was valid for me."

Emma gazed at him for a moment without speaking. He was sprawled out in his dear familiar way, his head back, his long legs stretched out in front of him, his hands thrust into his pockets.

"For four years," she said bravely, "you have seemed to me to be the most wonderful man — person — I have ever known. I have always felt though that I must guard against my feelings for you. They were too strong — they would blind me. Anyway, you evidently don't think much of me. You've just accused me of letting Kit Sundine make love to me."

"I thought at one time you were in love with him," Jonny said.

"I thought you were in love with Paola," Emma countered.

"Oh-h-h," Jonny made a great sighing noise. "She's a sweet girl and a lovely one and she had a schoolgirl crush on me until she met Arturo again. I thought that was plain for everyone to see. I didn't encourage it. That was also plain. I should have thought that even my cold, stony-hearted wife could have seen that."

"You did so much to build up the morale of your cold stony-hearted wife," said Emma. "You said I was like a maiden aunt once, you said I was like a ten-year-old child, that I was play-acting — "

"Let's not remember what I said," said Jonny. "You know perfectly well why I said those things. I wanted you — and you rebuffed me right from the beginning. 'This is purely a business proposition,' you said grandly. I will admit I was surprised. I had always had a sneaking feeling you were emotionally involved with me. But you were so young, I thought you would grow out of it. I was more convinced of it than ever when you said you would marry me. Perhaps I'm conceited. Anyway my conceit took a tumble, didn't it? You've done nothing but put me in my place ever since. I shall not forget the night you told me that however I had phrased my proposal, it would not have been acceptable to you."

"That was my pride coming to my rescue," said Emma. "No one wants to become a wife for the sake of expediency, for humdrum reasons."

"Would you like to know what I think of you now?" Jonny said quietly. "I want you more than ever, I think you're lovely and desirable and sweet and good — "

"I don't want flowery compliments," Emma said faintly.

"Those aren't compliments. They're statements of facts. I want you more than anything to be happy," Jonny said. He got up from the couch with a sudden lithe movement and walked over towards her. He put his hands in her hair and pulled it away from her face. "I'm going to make you love me," he said, "if I have to work twenty-four hours a day at it. And I'm not going to be pushed around any more with all this niminy-piminy stuff. We're going to be man and wife. You're going to be mine in every sense and like it." He bent forward and kissed her on the lips, hard, hungrily. Emma began to respond to his ardour and he drew away from her and looked down at her with luminous eyes. "There!" he said as though to a child. "That wasn't so unpleasant, was it?"

"Oh, Jonny," Emma pushed her head against his shirt front, and leaned against him as though he were something solid and dependable. "You've misunderstood me." He swung her up into his arms as though she were a doll and walked over to the couch with her and sat down with her on his lap.

"Mario will come in with the dinner," Emma protested.

"Let him," said Jonny. He began tracing her face with his forefinger. "Dear little face," he murmured, "such a cross, severe little face sometimes. So I misunderstood you, Emma. I should have been tough with you from the beginning and ignored your schoolgirl fancies."

"Love is not a schoolgirl fancy, Jonny," Emma whispered. "I wanted you to love me." She lay back in his arms, hardly believing in this happiness.

"I've always loved you," Jonny said. "Since you were sixteen. Why did I get you your job? So that you would be near to me. Why were you the first person I thought of when I won the prize?"

"But you didn't know you loved me then — if you did," said Emma.

"Yes, I loved you," Jonny said, "but it was a tranquil, taken for granted, emotion. It was our friend Kit who blew it up into a blazing fire. He showed me the way the wind was blowing when he nearly drove me mad with jealousy after the *palio*. Then I began to wonder what was the matter with me. What has this little witch done to me, I thought. What am I shivering and shaking for over little Emma? I didn't give in too easily. It was difficult admission to make, that I was irrevocably, inconsolably in love with you, especially when you seemed to hate the very sight of me. When did you begin to find me less repulsive, Emma? I have a sneaking feeling you enjoyed our kiss just now."

Emma looked into his eyes, dark, melting, and felt as though she were drowning in exquisite happiness. "I've always loved you," she whispered. "I've always longed more than anything for your kisses."

Jonny bent his face over hers. "I love you, too, my darling Emma," he said, "we're going to have a marvellous life together. Should we get married again — in church? To show we mean it for ever? For eternity? Perhaps we could find a little English church in Florence?"

"I would like that," Emma said.

There was a sound on the terrace and Mario entered with their dinner. He busied himself tactfully with the table as Emma slipped out of Jonny's arms.

"Oh, Mario," Jonny said, when the man had finished serving them, "I wonder if you would take my suitcase upstairs." He indicated his week-end bag which was still by the door where he had dropped it on first entering the studio. "It seems to have got left down here by mistake."

He looked at Emma, his dark eyes

demanding and eloquent with love. In a voice that only she could hear, he said, "There are no divisions in this house any more."

# THE END

*Other titles in the*
*Ulverscroft Large Print Series:*

## TO FIGHT THE WILD
### Rod Ansell and Rachel Percy

Lost in uncharted Australian bush, Rod Ansell survived by hunting and trapping wild animals, improvising shelter and using all the bushman's skills he knew.

## COROMANDEL
### Pat Barr

India in the 1830s is a hot, uncomfortable place, where the East India Company still rules. Amelia and her new husband find themselves caught up in the animosities which seethe between the old order and the new.

## THE SMALL PARTY
### Lillian Beckwith

A frightening journey to safety begins for Ruth and her small party as their island is caught up in the dangers of armed insurrection.

## THE WILDERNESS WALK
### Sheila Bishop

Stifling unpleasant memories of a misbegotten romance in Cleave with Lord Francis Aubrey, Lavinia goes on holiday there with her sister. The two women are thrust into a romantic intrigue involving none other than Lord Francis.


## THE RELUCTANT GUEST
### Rosalind Brett

Ann Calvert went to spend a month on a South African farm with Theo Borland and his sister. They both proved to be different from her first idea of them, and there was Storr Peterson — the most disturbing man she had ever met.


## ONE ENCHANTED SUMMER
### Anne Tedlock Brooks

A tale of mystery and romance and a girl who found both during one enchanted summer.

## CLOUD OVER MALVERTON
### Nancy Buckingham

Dulcie soon realises that something is seriously wrong at Malverton, and when violence strikes she is horrified to find herself under suspicion of murder.

## AFTER THOUGHTS
### Max Bygraves

The Cockney entertainer tells stories of his East End childhood, of his RAF days, and his post-war showbusiness successes and friendships with fellow comedians.

## MOONLIGHT
## AND MARCH ROSES
### D. Y. Cameron

Lynn's search to trace a missing girl takes her to Spain, where she meets Clive Hendon. While untangling the situation, she untangles her emotions and decides on her own future.

## NURSE ALICE IN LOVE
### Theresa Charles

Accepting the post of nurse to little Fernie Sherrod, Alice Everton could not guess at the romance, suspense and danger which lay ahead at the Sherrod's isolated estate.

## POIROT INVESTIGATES
### Agatha Christie

Two things bind these eleven stories together — the brilliance and uncanny skill of the diminutive Belgian detective, and the stupidity of his Watson-like partner, Captain Hastings.

## LET LOOSE THE TIGERS
### Josephine Cox

Queenie promised to find the long-lost son of the frail, elderly murderess, Hannah Jason. But her enquiries threatened to unlock the cage where crucial secrets had long been held captive.

## THE TWILIGHT MAN
### Frank Gruber

Jim Rand lives alone in the California desert awaiting death. Into his hermit existence comes a teenage girl who blows both his past and his brief future wide open.

## DOG IN THE DARK
### Gerald Hammond

Jim Cunningham breeds and trains gun dogs, and his antagonism towards the devotees of show spaniels earns him many enemies. So when one of them is found murdered, the police are on his doorstep within hours.

## THE RED KNIGHT
### Geoffrey Moxon

When he finds himself a pawn on the chessboard of international espionage with his family in constant danger, Guy Trent becomes embroiled in moves and countermoves which may mean life or death for Western scientists.